Innocent Redemption

June Cianci Flori

Innocent Redemption
Copyright © 2021 June Cianci Flori

Produced and printed by Stillwater River Publications.
All rights reserved. Written and produced in the
United States of America. This book may not be reproduced
or sold in any form without the expressed, written
permission of the author(s) and publisher.

Visit our website at
www.StillwaterPress.com
for more information.

First Stillwater River Publications Edition

ISBN: 978-1-955123-46-4

1 2 3 4 5 6 7 8 9 10
Written by June Cianci Flori
Cover painting by June Cianci Flori
Published by Stillwater River Publications,
Pawtucket, RI, USA.

I dedicate this book to my dear George for his love, devotion, inspiration, and encouragement in all my endeavors, and he always made me feel so special.

Acknowledgements

Many thanks and much love to my wonderful granddaughter, Rachel, for all the time, work, and patience she gave helping to publish this book. Her consciencious devotion to the task made this book possible. Thank you!

INNOCENT REDEMPTION

One
———

A ngelina Tramonti was born on a very hot day in July. Her mother
Philomena was relieved to be of the burden since this was her
third birth and it was a sweltering summer. Having had two sons in
the previous two years, this child was her first daughter. Angelina was
a docile baby which was in her favor because her mother's time was
almost completely taken up with household chores and cooking. Her
husband, Antonio, was a stonemason. After a hard day laying bricks,
he would come home tired and hungry looking for a hot meal.

Angelina was a pleasant-looking baby with even features, none of
which would be considered outstanding. She had light, grey-green
eyes, a small nose and a thin-lipped mouth. The bone structure of
her face was flat with no definite cheekbones. However, as she grew
older, her facial features filled out. Also, being petite in stature, she
could be considered cute and attractive.

The Tramonti home, located in Little Italy in the Federal Hill sec-
tion of Providence, Rhode Island, was what one would consider an
upper-middle-class cottage in the late 1800's. It consisted of four large
bedrooms and bath on the second floor. A large kitchen, an ample
storage closet, and a double parlor made up the first floor. The house
was heated by two large fireplaces in the parlor and kitchen and lit

by gas lamps on the walls. A porch, which was used in the heat of the summer when and if anyone had time to sit, graced the front of the house. Antonio Tramonti was a handsome man of tall stature with strong chiseled features. He was proud of his home which he was able to maintain without much difficulty because he earned a good pay as a stonemason. He and his wife had come from Italy together with their respective families who had been friends for generations. They were both in their teens at that time and the marriage was more-or-less arranged, although they did love each other. They were a very close couple and seemed to enjoy each others company. Philomena was as short as he was tall. She did not reach five feet, had very plain features, but her coloring of auburn hair and bright blue eyes made her somewhat attractive.

By the time Angelina reached the age of six, her mother had given birth to three other children—a boy named Giuseppe and two girls, Philomena and Carlotta. Angelina being the oldest daughter, was put into service cooking and cleaning and taking care of the younger children. Her two older brothers Costantino and Antonio, Jr. had to help maintain the outside of the home, the yard, and had the responsibilty of making sure there was enough wood for the fireplaces in winter. Sometimes they had to help their father when he had a big job laying tile. They and Angelina went to school as often as it was possible.

Being a family of eight, the children learned from an early age to be frugal, do their chores, and not expect too many material things. They were grateful for a couple of clean outfits, a decent pair of shoes, and a hot meal at the end of the day. In spite of their lean lifestyle, they were a very close, happy family, bonding even more because of their hardships. In fact, they felt as though they were a cut above the other Italian families in their neighborhood because their mother Philomena had lived near Rome before coming to this country and spoke the true Italian language. Most of the Italian immigrants who spoke with dialects couldn't understand her. In their opinion this made her special.

Sometime on a Sunday in the summer, the family would pack a big lunch, put on their bathing suits, pile into Antonio's truck and head for a nearby beach. This was such a special occasion for them. It was almost the only event they did for the whole year. Their father Antonio, loved the water. He would go way out beyond the surf and swim to his hearts content. It was a beautiful, perfect Sunday when the family arrived on the beach. The childen played at the edge of the water. Philomina sat on a blanket not far from them and as usual Antonio dove in and swam out beyond the waves. Philomina kept a watchful eye on the children always counting heads. From far out in the ocean Antonio waved to Philomena. She happily waved back. He was really enjoying himself. Again he waved and she waved back. When he waved the third time, only half his arm came out of the water. Was something wrong? Was the wave a signal of distress? Philomena jumped up. She ran to the water's edge. The children noticed her anxiety. They followed her troubled gaze out to where their father was swimming. They could not see him. Where was he? Suddenly only one of his hands appeared for a a second, then disappeared. Hardly breathing, they waited for another sign. There was a slight ripple. Then the water was still. Nothing was moving. Philomena started screaming calling Antonio's name. She ran into the water. The children were crying for their father. It was too late. Antonio had succumbed to the sea he loved.

Life as the Tramonti family knew it was to change forever.

Two

The days of mourning Antonio for his wife and children dragged on for months. They were all in a state of numbness. They didn't want to believe he was gone. It was not true. They expected him to come to the table for supper at any time. Philomena was in a state of shock. Her brain could not manage her everyday obligations to her family. She was left with six children to care for and no means of supporting them. Her oldest child was twelve and the youngest two. Her sister Concetta and her husband Guido had come forward and paid for Antonio's funeral. She was now indebted to them. She had to struggle to get her thoughts together and try to be strong for her children. She had to deal with reality.

Her two oldest sons, Costantino and Antonio, Jr. went to work every day after school with their Uncle Guido who was a tile setter. They helped cut tiles, swept floors, and anything else that was needed. They each earned ten cents a week. This was given to their mother for household expenses. Angelina, who was eight, went through the neighborhood with a broom offering to sweep people's front steps and sidewalks. She did a thorough job, paying attention to the corners and cracks. Sometimes she would get a few pennies. If she was really lucky, a nickel. Philomena started taking in laundry. A big tub in the basement was filled with water one pail at a time from a small sink. A load of clothes would be washed using a scrubbing board and lye soap. Each piece of clothing had to be wrung out by hand. The tub, still very heavy with water, had to be carried out into the yard and emptied. Again it had to be refilled to rinse the clothes. After the clothes were rinsed and wrung out again, they were brought outside and hung on the line to dry. Some had to be ironed after drying. This was a very exhausting chore for Philomena. She was a small woman, and it was difficult for her to lift the tub and the heavy wet clothes. Also, her hands were rubbed raw and bleeding. She charged twenty-five cents a load, so the more loads she could do in a day meant more money in her pocket.

In spite of all their efforts to support the household, it was barely enough to eke out a living. It was difficult to feed six hungry children. Again her sister, Concetta, and her husband came forward to help. They had a proposition. They were financially well off, and their biggest disappointment was they were unable to have children. They offered to take little Carlotta and bring her up as their own. However, she would always know who her mother was. This was a heartbreaking decision for Philomena. She didn't want her youngest daughter growing up apart from the family. However, Carlotta would have every advantage living with them. A way of life she knew she could never give her. With a heavy heart and some relief, she agreed to their offer. They promised to bring Carlotta to visit every week so she would never forget them.

Carlotta, or Lotty as she was called, was not happy to have to live with Aunt Concetta and Uncle Guido. She wanted to grow up with her family and mother. She was educated in the best of schools, wore the finest clothes, took piano lessons, and was doted on. All these advantages didn't matter to her. She still resented them for taking her away from her family. Furthermore, she didn't really like her Aunt and Uncle. They were old-fashioned in their thinking and watched over her to the point of suffocation because of their responsibilty in caring for her. Lotty held this resentment against them to her dying day. When she was an adult, she purposely distanced herself from them, and took pleasure knowing they were hurt and disappointed.

However, Angelina was very envious of Lotty. Why couldn't she have been the one they had chosen to live with them? She always wanted nice clothes and the finer things in life. Being the oldest daughter, she was relegated to menial household chores, sweeping sidewalks, and hand-me-down clothes. She would always resent Lotty for her advantages.

Even with Lotty gone and everyone doing their best to contribute to the family's income, it still wasn't enough to sustain them. Philomena had to think of some other means of income. She thought of something she could do. It would have a great impact on her children and their way of life. She couldn't worry about that. If it meant survival, it must be done. She started making plans.

Three

After Antonio's death, Philomena had received a letter of sympathy from his cousin Rocco who lived in Genoa. At that time he had expressed his desire to come to this country. Before this could happen, he had to save up enough money for his passage, have a sponsor, a job, and a place to live. At this time, many immigrants were coming to this country and they had to fulfill these requirements. Some were single. Many were married, and they were working to save enough money to send for their wives and children. It was mandatory they have a place to live or they would not be accepted. Philomena could take advantage of this requirement—she had the place for them to live.

She wrote to Rocco and offered him her home when he was ready to come to this country. To her surprise, he answered almost immediately. He was very happy with her offer. In fact, he had planned to ask Antonio this favor, but after her husband's death, he didn't want to impose on her. Now, they could make their plans. Rocco would be arriving in a month.

The news of Rocco's immigration to America spread quickly in his paese. Some of his friends and relatives also wanted to come to this country and asked Rocco to write to Philomena asking if she had room for them also. Of course, Philomena was only too happy to accommodate as many boarders as possible. The more boarders, the more money. She told Rocco she had the perfect set-up. Four large bedrooms for sleeping, and a large kitchen for eating. Rocco could feel free to bring his friend. Rocco arrived within a month. He brought with him his friend Sylvio. Both had jobs as laborers and were sponsored by their boss. Philomena and her children welcomed them with a hot meal and a warm bed. Her two sons who had occupied that bedroom had to double up with their younger brother Giuseppe.

Two months later, a father and son, the Branos from Roccamonfina arrived, followed by Bruno and Georgio from Mont San Appio. Philomena had room for only two more boarders in the last of the four bedrooms. This was soon filled with the arrival of Giuseppe and Thomase Verdi from Naples. With eight boarders each paying ten dollars a week, it was a comfortable income for the Tramonti family. Philomena was proud her plan had worked.

Of course now with all their bedrooms taken over by boarders, much to their dislike, the children were relegated to the basement. Philomena slept on a cot in the living-room so she would be available when the boarders came down for breakfast. Angelina was very unhappy sleeping in the cellar. She missed her nice warm bed she had shared with her sister Philomena. The old, hard mattress she had to sleep on was a poor sustitute. She no longer had a dresser for her clothes, but had to keep them in cardboard boxes. She didn't like all these big, burly, smelly, men infiltrating her house, taking over the kitchen table half the night, talking, playing cards and drinking beer and wine. She had to clean up after them, make their beds in the morning and help wash the tremendous piles of dirty clothes that smelled as bad as they did.

Her younger sister, Philomena or Mena as she was called, was very beautiful. She soon became aware at a young age, judging by the lustful looks some of the boarders gave her, that her beauty could be a powerful tool in raising her position in society. She liked to stay in the kitchen at night and watch the men talk, drink and bask in their admiring glances. By listening, she found out what was going on in their world, how they felt about women, and what their future plans were. She also learned some not-so-nice Italian words that came in handy during her lifetime at appropriate moments. After the men were done for the evening, she and Angelina would clean the table and prepare it for breakfast. Much to Angelina's disgust, Mena delighted in finishing up any wine, beer or liquor left in their glasses. Mena also knew all about the males' private parts because she had peeked into their bedrooms at night when they were undressing, or in the bathoom when they got out of the tub. When she tried to describe them to Angelina, she was told to shut up and she should be ashamed of herself. Angelina was no fun, boring and dull.

Angelina hated her existence. She liked the finer things in life. She didn't like the coarse, crude way of living imposed on her. There was only one way out. She knew what it was. She was determind to make it happen.

Four

Angelina was not her mother's favorite. Philomena would get angry with her because she was always sneaking off somewhere to read a book instead of doing her chores. She was envious of anyone who seemed to be getting more than her share at dinner or anywhere else. Philomena knew her daughter was a grabby person, always comparing what others had—always wanting a little more than was due her. This was only one of the reasons Angelina rubbed her the wrong way.

Angelina was not too pleased with her mother either. Whenever she had a few minutes to herself, which wasn't very often, she would hide in a closet or behind a door to read a few pages in a book. It wasn't long before her mother would find her and angrily order her back to work. She and her brothers and sister spoke English. But the boarders and her mother only spoke Italian, so her family had to speak the language to converse with them. This bothered her because Angelina wanted to speak English as she had learned in school. She wanted to be considered American.

As the boarders were able to move out and get on with their lives, they would leave, but another would soon take their place. Philomena was a no-nonsense landlady. She was a small, bullish woman. In fact sometimes her face resembled a bulldog. She set the rules of the house. The big burly men followed. They had to buy their own food and she would cook it. That way every man ate what he liked. Each boarder was allowed only two baths a week and only one bath towel. Laundry was measured by the piece. If anyone had over six pieces of dirty clothes a week, they were charged five cents per extra. Bedding was changed on a rotating basis once a month. Breakfast was served at seven a. m., and supper at six p. m. Rent was paid on the first of the month. Philomena was so involved in running her boarding house, she had little time to pay attention to her children. As Mena once said, "We weren't brought up, we were drug up."

The years of boarders coming and going seemed to go on forever. Angelina went from a girl of twelve to a young lady of seventeen. Her two older brothers had become successful in the tile business after working with their Uncle Guido and brought in a good pay every week Her oldest brother Costantino had taken on the role of head-of-the-house, and the children respected his position.

Giuseppe still worked for a stone mason. He made headstones for graves and learned the art of engraving the names and dates on them. His future was secure. Mena had her share of boyfriends. They took her to fancy restaurants and parties. She learned how the more priviledged lived, how they decorated their homes, dressed and entertained. She too came to like the finer things in life. She became a fountain of knowledge for Angelina feeding the craving she already had to better herself.

As boarders left they were not replaced. The family was coming into its own. Angelina's time to leave was imminent. She was no longer an asset, but was beginning to become a liability. Time to put her plan into action. Time to make another trip to that tailor shop.

Five
——

Augustino Rossi was a handsome man of twenty-five years, the oldest of three children. He lived with his parents, Carmella and Pasquale Jr. and his brother Paolo, and sister, Concetta. They lived a very comfortable life in a small seven-room bungalow on Ring St. just off the busy main street of Atwells Ave. Augustino's grandparents, Pasquale Sr. and and his wife, Giovanina owned the house and also lived with them. Pasquale Sr. also owned a block of ten stores on Atwells Ave. One of the stores was occupied by Augustino's father as his tailor shop. Augustino had learned to be a tailor from his father and worked with him. They did all types of tailoring from alterations to custom-made suits. They also sold sewing supplies.

Among their steady customers, a young girl in the neighborhood had been coming in lately to buy thread. Augustino found her quite attractive with her auburn hair and light blue eyes. She had an air of quiet refinement about her that appealed to him. After making her purchase, she would always stay a few minutes longer and have a light conversation mostly about the weather. It impressed him when she bought anything from a spool of thread or a package of needles; she always made sure she got the most for her money—very sensible. She piqued his interest.

He would have to start inquiring around the neighborhood in a subtle way to find out what her name was and where she lived. How could he go about getting to know her better? If he found out where she lived, would he have the nerve to go to her house? Would he be welcomed or turned away? These questions went round and round in his head until he could think of nothing else. Finally he felt compelled to find the answers.

Early Sunday morning, right after attending mass, he started his quest by walking the neighborhood, looking for people who might give him some information. Would he be brave enough to go ahead with his plans after he found out what he wanted to know?

Augustino didn't need to have put himself through all this self-imposed torture. Angelina was taking care of it. She had already set the process in motion.

Six

Angelina washed and curled her hair, applied her lipstick carefully, rubbed some on her cheeks for color, put on her best dress, and set out on her mission. She had been going to Rossi's Tailor shop on Atwells Ave. to buy sewing supplies for about six months. The young man, Augustino, who was the owner's son, had always waited on her. He was very handsome and seemed interested in talking with her. She found him very attractive not only because of his looks, but also he was a man of means. He had a good job. His family owned a nice bungalow and a row of ten stores, one housing the tailor shop. They were financially stable. This was very appealing to her.

Up until now, there had never been any conversation of significance between them, so he did not know too much about her. She had not been forthcoming with any personal information. Her tactics were going to change. If he had any interest in her at all, he would have all the information needed to further the relationship.

Augustino was still agonizing about how he would get to know more about the young woman customer, when to his delight and surprise, she was entering the shop. His prayers had been answered. She looked especially attractive today—with her face slightly flushed, shiny auburn hair, and glistening blue eyes. He quickly went to the counter. His heart started to beat faster.

When Angelina entered the shop she could see that Augustino was happy to see her. His face lit up. It was almost as if he had been anticipating her arrival.

He came immediatly to the counter. She looked up at him with a shy little smile and a long sideways glance—something she had learned by watching her sister, Mena, who had no trouble attracting men. After making her purchase, she lingered and said with a smile, "I've been coming here for quite a while and never really introduced myself. I'm Angelina Tramonti."

He quickly replied, "And I'm Augustino Rossi. My pleasure."

The conversation then turned toward the weather, and this gave her another opening. "Thank goodness it is a nice day, because if I had to walk all the way from my house in the rain, it wouldn't be very pleasant."

He answered just the way Angelina hoped he would. "Why, do you live far from here? "

Angelina answered, "Oh, not that far, only about three blocks away at 41 Spruce St. It's the big brown cottage with a porch across the front."

Augustino was amazed that all the information he was trying to obtain, was coming to him without any effort on his part. Almost a miracle! The conversation then turned to local events and the church festival next weekend.

Angelina casually let him know she would be going with her sister, Mena. They always watched the parade from the church steps.

Augustino was enthralled and was so grateful Angelina had given him all this information he was looking for without her even realizing it.

After a few last pleasantries, Angelina said goodbye with a big smile leaving Augustino in somewhat of a daze. She walked home with a satisfied little smile on her face. She had planted the seed. Now it was time for Augustino to grow the relationship. Would he?

Seven

The day of the Mt. Carmel Church Festival dawned bright and sunny. Crowds formed along the sides of the street to watch the procession. Male parishioners carried the statue of the Blessed Virgin Mary on their shoulders. They were followed by the Church Pastor, city councilmen, representatives, and groups of firemen and policemen. The local boy scout troop marched to the rousing beat of the high school band. Various other organizations followed, making the procession at least an hour long. The street was lined with vendors selling their wares.

Angelina and her sister, Mena, made their way through the crowd to the church steps where they could sit and still see the procedings. Angelina'a gaze went back and forth searching the crowd for a sign of Augustino. Would he come? The procession was coming to an end soon and there was still no sign of him. Had all her hints gone unnoticed, or was he just not interested?

Suddenly, Angelina saw him weaving his way through the crowd. As he was approaching, she could see he was searching the people on the steps—hopefully for her. She wasn't taking any chances he would not find her and turn back. She waved to him and called his name. He waved back with a big smile and made his way toward her. Their eyes met for a short but very meaningful moment. Angelina's heart did an extra beat.

She quickly introduced him to her sister, Mena. Mena, who was only sixteen, knew more about men than Angelina. She gave him the once-over and decided she approved. He had a lean, muscular physique and looked very handsome in a blue shirt and white slacks. His shiny-black hair was well cut and slicked back making his look complete.

After shaking hands with Mena, he sat down between them. Conversation came easily commenting on the beautiful day and the procession.

Augustino was thrilled he had been so clever in finding out so much information about Angelina. He didn't know if he would have the nerve to approach her at the church and was hesitant to do so. He didn't want to seem too forward. Finally, when the procession was almost over, he decided to take his chances. Now, to his delight, he was sitting between Angelina and her sister, Mena. Mena was very beautiful, but Angelina held a special charm for him. After a short conversation, he offered to buy them some refreshments which they readily accepted.

After enjoying a doughboy each, things were quieting down at the festival and they started toward home. After walking a short distance, Mena excused herself saying she had to see a friend. She knew Angelina wanted some time alone with Augustino.

Augustino and Angelina were finally by themselves. Their eyes met again, and Augustino tentatively took her hand. They walked along in silence, not having to say a word, just enjoying each other's company.

As they approached Angelina's house, her brother Costantino couldn't believe what he was seeing—Angelina walking and holding hands with a strange man! His temper flared! He let out a shrill whistle, a sign for her to get home immediately.

It sent a chill through Angelina. She knew she was in big trouble.

Augustino was horrified. He should have known better to never hold hands with a young girl he had not been properly introduced to.

Angelina was embarrassed.

They quickly said goodbye.

Augustino looked at her longingly feeling he would never see her again. He could see the fear in her eyes.

Angelina entered the house and ran into the pantry pretending to get a drink. She could hear her brother, Costentino entering the kitchen. He was coming toward her. His steps were getting closer. Her heart beat faster. It was a moment of dread. She feared what she was in for. She would soon find out.

Eight

Hoping to escape her brother's wrath, Angelina had run into the pantry. She stood there rigid with fear. She could hear her brother Costantino's footsteps coming closer. The hair on her neck began to tingle. Suddenly his hand was on her shoulder, spinning her around. She saw the rage in his eyes. She made a run for the stairs and the safety of her bed. She didn't get far when her brother's hands were on her neck.

He kept shouting, "Who is he? Who is he?" while banging her head against the wall with every step.

She reached her bed and threw herself on her back. She raised her legs and used her feet to ward off any further attacks.

He was unrelenting asking, "Who is he? Who is he?"

She was afraid to give him Augustino's name for fear he would do him harm. Her fear suddenly turned to courage and she said in a steady voice, "If you don't stop attacking me, I will not tell you his name."

Her brother was stunned at her remark and seemed to snap out of his rage.

She then made up a fake name to satisfy him.

He turned and slowly left the room.

Angelina lay in bed completely drained. It was summer and all the windows were open. The whole neighborhood must have heard what happened. She could not face anyone again. What had been a beautiful, innocent moment had been turned into something ugly

When Mena came home and found out what had happened, she couldn't believe Angelina had been so foolish coming close to the house holding hands with Augustino. She had many a liason with young men but was smart enough to never get caught.

Angelina stayed alone and depressed in her bed for three days. She couldn't face the world. She thought of Augustino. What must he think of her brother? Had he heard what had happened to her? It made her sick to think she would never see him again. What man would want to deal with someone like Costantino?

If her mother knew what had happened, it didn't seem to bother her. If Angelina had been punished, she probably deserved it. She was annoyed with Angelina only because she was staying in bed and not doing her chores. She would put a stop to this foolishness. After three days, she descended into the basement and in her bullish way ordered Angelina to get up and get back to work.

Not another word was ever spoken about the incident.

When she saw Costantino, he just looked at her as if nothing had happened. The only one she could find some comfort in was Mena. Mena didn't give her much sympathy, mostly criticising her for being so dumb to get caught.

Meanwhile, Augustino was beside himself. He felt terribly guilty for getting Angelina in trouble. He wondered what had happened to her. Was she all right? He knew her brother was furious. He had to make it right for Angelina. He would approach her brother and explain to him he cared about Angelina and would never take advantage of her. It was just an innocent walk home from the festival. Would her brother see him? Would he accept his apology or attack him? He had to take the chance not only for Angelina, but for his own reputation. He would go to their house next Sunday when Costantino should be home and try to straighten things out. He wanted to see Angelina again.

On Sunday, Augustino, with a lump in his throat and fear in his heart, climbed the stairs to the porch of the Tramonti home. He rang the bell. A small-bullish-looking woman, who he figured must be Angelina's mother, answered the door. He introduced himself and asked if Costantino was home.

She invited him in and called for her son.

As Costantino entered the room, he recognized the man as the one walking with Angelina. He could feel the rage boiling in him. How did he have the nerve to show his face in this house? Before confronting him, he went to his room, opened the bureau drawer and took out his gun.

Nine

Before he walked toward Augustino, Costantino put the gun in his back pocket. To his surprise, Augustino offered him his hand and politely introduced himself. He apologized profusely for overstepping his bounds with Angelina. He had a deep respect for her and would never take advantage of their friendship. Costantino could see how sincere he was in his apology.

He asked Augustino how he had become acquainted with Angelina. Had they been having secret meetings?

Augustino told him how Angelina had come to his tailor shop many times to buy sewing supplies. Augustino explained he was a tailor working with his father in their shop on Atwells Ave. It was one in a row of ten stores his family owned on that block.

Costantino started hearing better. He asked Augustino where he lived.

Augustino explained he lived with his parents right behind the stores on Ring Street.

Costantino glanced over at his mother who was sitting in the room listening to the conversation. They gave each other a knowing glance. Here was a gentleman of means. Augustino was getting more interesting by the moment. He could be a wonderful catch for

Angelina. She would have a good home. Maybe she would be able to fulfill some of her greediness. She was always comparing what she had with other people. She had to have the best or more than anyone else. Her mother was tired of Angelina's ways. If she could marry this young man, it would be good for everyone involved. They would be relieved of supporting her. Philomena glanced back at Costantino with an encouraging smirk.

Costantino now became more congenial toward Augustino. He praised him for having the decency to come forward and apologize. He told him if Angelina wanted to see him again, he would be welcome to call on her.

Augustino was thrilled that he had been able to convince Costantino of his sincerety. He was proud of himself for being brave enough to face him. He had carefully chosen his words to impress him, and it had worked!

Now Costantino asked Augustino if he would like to see Angelina. She hadn't been feeling too well lately, and maybe seeing him would make her feel better. Augustino couldn't agree fast enough. He was going to see his precious Angelina again. Another miracle!

Costantino motioned to his mother to find Angelina and bring her to the living room.

Angelina had heard Augustino's arrival. She couldn't believe he had the courage to come to her home. She had seen Costantino get his gun. She hid behind the bedroom door hardly able to breathe—expecting to hear gun shots any moment. She feared for Augustino. She overheard their conversation and to her surprise it had gone well. Augustino was so clever knowing how to get on the right side of her brother. Now her mother was calling her into the living room. It truly was a miracle!

When Angelina entered the living room, she wanted to run to Augustino. Their eyes met as they gazed longingly at each other.

Costantino told Angelina about his conversation with Augustino and how impressed he was with his bravery and honesty.

Even though Angelina had overheard the conversation, she smiled to show her approval at the outcome.

Costantino now told Augustino he and his mother gave their approval for him to call on Angelina at least once a week if he so desired. They could visit on the porch or the living room.

Angelina and Augustino were thrilled at the news. Augustino thanked Costantino for granting him this priviledge. With a big smile he said his goodbyes. Looking lovingly at Angelina he said, "If it is all right with you, I will be back next Sunday."

She answered, "I will be so happy to see you."

Augustino left the Tramonti home feeling a surge of happiness flow through him. He couldn't wait to get home and tell his family about the wonderful girl he was going to visit.

Augustino had no idea what was going to happen when he told his parents the good news!

Ten

Augustino approached his house with joyful anticipation. He couldn't believe he had won the approval of Angelina's brother and mother. He was anxious to share his happiness with his parents.

The Rossi family lived in a good-sized bungalow on Ring St. in Providence. It was considered medium-upper-class—well maintained and fashionable. Augustino's parents had emigrated from Italy when they were in their teens, married young, and had worked tirelessly to reach their present status in life. Carmella had worked in the mill as a weaver, and her husband, Pasquale, Jr. learned his trade as a tailor by working with his father, Pasquale, Sr. Augustino's grandparents owned the house they all lived in and the stores housing the tailor shop. The family was more well-off than most people of their generation.

Carmella was tall and slim with beady brown eyes, a prominent nose and thin grim lips giving her a hawkish look which could be intimidating. She was very protective of her children and wanted the best for them. She was proud of the hard work she had done to help them gain their present status in life.

Her husband, Pasquale, Sr. was equally proud of his achievements and expected his children to have an even better life than his.

Carmella was standing at the kitchen window when she saw her son, Augustino coming up the walk. He was in a hurry and had a look of anticipation on his face. Hopefully, he had some good news.

Augustino burst through the back door, kissed his mother hello, and asked for his father. Carmella directed him to the living room where his father was reading the newspaper. Augustino asked his father to stop what he was doing because he had some good news for both of them.

He then told them in an excited voice about the wonderful girl he had met. How thrilled he was to have been accepted by her family and was allowed to visit her twice a week. He then went on to describe how beautiful she was and how attracted he was to her.

Of course his parents wanted to know all about this wonderful girl. Who was she? What was her name? Where did she live? How did they meet?

When Augustino told them her name was Angelina Tramonti, her parents looked as though they had been shot at close range. His mother gave an audible gasp. His father leaned close to him and with bulging eyes and an angry voice said, "How can you lower yourself to want to be with someone from the Tramonti family? They had to take in boarders. She has been exposed to living with rough immigrants. How much culture and refinement can she have?"

His mother added, "We want someone better for you. Someone we can be proud of to be your wife and have our grandchildren. It would be a great disappointment if you got involved with someone of her background."

Augustino was shocked at his parents' reaction. He explained Angelina was a kind, wonderful person. She was refined and cultured. It wasn't her fault her father had drowned and they had to take in boarders. He wanted to be with her. She made him happy. Maybe if they met her they would understand and be more accepting.

His parents were adamant. They let him know they were against him if he continued seeing THAT girl. If he were younger, they would have forbade him, but being of age, they could not control his actions. His father even hinted about him losing his inheritance.

Augustino was completely deflated. He couldn't believe his parents would react in such a way. They had taken away much of his happiness. He would not let them stop him from seeing her.

Every Wednesday evening and Sunday afternoon Augustino went to visit Angelina. They would usually sit on the porch holding hands and talking about their feelings for one another. Sometimes they would take walks to a nearby park where they could be alone and exchange passionate kisses. Angelina's family welcomed Augustino into their family. Soon he became a steady guest at their Sunday dinner table. Things were getting serious. Augustino was anxious to give Angelina an engagement ring. When that happened, he would have to be ready for a standoff with his family.

Angelina wondered why she had never met Augustino's family. He had never suggested taking her to his home. Was he afraid they would not accept her? Did they even know she existed?

Augustino's parents realized every Wednesday and Sunday when Augustino was not at home, he was with that Tramonti girl. This had been going on for several months. There seemed to be no way of changing his mind. It might be a smart move at this time to make him feel they have accepted his decision. Maybe ask to meet her—get to know something about her. Maybe he will see she doesn't fit in with his family's lifestyle. If that doesn't work and it appears he is intent on marrying her, Pasquale would have to implement the plan he knows would stop the marriage.

Eleven

When Carmella and Pasquale, Jr. realized Augustino was not going to stop seeing Angelina, they decided it was time to change their tactics. They thought sometimes when you accept a situation, it may soften a person's rebellious attitude. Maybe if they seemed to be accepting Angelina, Augustino wouldn't be so adamant in his determination to keep this relationship. They started their new idea by asking Augustino to invite Angelina for coffee on one of the Wednesday afternoons.

Augustino was thrilled his parents were finally realizing how serious he was. He couldn't wait to pass the invitation along to Angelina.

She was happy the long-awaited invitation had finally arrived. She also realized if they had waited this long to see her, they were proably hoping Augustino would lose interest and the meeting would never happen. Now, after all this time, they were more or less forced into the situation. When she told her mother and brother Costantino about the invitation, they were very pleased and urged her to go. It was as if they were waiting for this moment more than she was.

On the following Wednesday, Angelina, accompanied Augustino to meet his parents. He seemed estatic. She wasn't. She felt he was somewhat naive about the reason his parents had put forth this invitation. It would be interesting to see how they welcomed her. She felt she was on trial.

Angelina's intuition was right. Augustino's parents were anxious to meet her so they could find some flaw or characteristic in her they could make Augustino aware of. They didn't realize what they were dealing with in Angelina.

Angelina was her most charming self. She had dressed impeccably, her hair and makeup looked professionally done. She extended her hand gracefully and smiled sweetly when introduced to his parents. She was sure his parents felt she was below their standards. It was up to her to make them change their minds.

His mother accepted her handshake and said she was so happy they had finally met. Her lips were smiling. Her eyes were not. They were cold. They told her true feelings.

Angelina felt his mother could be intimidating. She was tall, so when she spoke, she looked down at Angelina. Her face had a severe expression. She would be hard to deal with.

His father, on the other hand, was a pleasant-looking man, quite attractive, and seemed more congenial. His eyes were warm. He welcomed her with an embrace and led her into the dining-room where coffee and pastries were being served.

Carmella was very observant of Angelina. She wasn't beautiful, but very attractive, well-dressed, and makeup. Since Carmella and her husband were not very fluent in English, Angelina spoke to them in perfect Italian. She could be very charming. This was not a naive little shop girl. She was putting her best foot forward to impress them. She could be manipulative and cunning. Carmella observed how Angelina was looking at all the expensive china on the table, the fine furniture, rugs and draperies. Oh yes, this girl was after more than just Augustino. However she could not find a single flaw in her behavior. To Augustino she seemed perfect. She could see how much in love he was. He was always gazing at her and putting his arm around her. This was going to be a problem. Could they interfere in this relationship and break their son's heart?

Pasquale was very impressed with Angelina. He could see how Augustino had fallen under her spell. She seemed to have no faults. She could carry on an intelligent conversation in English or Italian. He could tell by his wife's attitude she was upset things were going so well.

Angelina was very proud of her behavior. It had gone just the way she planned. Her sister, Mena, who was more worldly-wise, had given her some helpful tips on how to speak and act. She found their home to be definitely high-class with all the lovely things she wanted to have some day. She loved Augustino and his love for her would make it possible to obtain these possessions. Even if his parents didn't approve, she would make it happen.

At the end of the evening they said their goodbyes. It seemed like it had been a very gracious and productive meeting. Angelina and Augustino walked away holding hands.

Augustino was thrilled it had gone so well.

Angelina was thrilled it had gone just as she had planned.

After saying goodby for the last time, Pasquale, Jr. closed the door. He looked at his wife's grief-stricken face. He gave her a little smile and a wink and said, "Don't worry, it will be taken care of."

Twelve

Angelina's family was happy to hear her visit with Augustino's parents had gone well. Now was it time for the parents to meet? Why waste time? Let's keep this relationship moving.

Angelina was mortified thinking about Mr. and Mrs. Rossi coming to visit. Her home didn't meet their standards. The furnishings were old and out-dated. They had no fancy china or linens. The one good point was everything from ceiling to floor was clean and polished.

The written invitaton was given to Augustino who delivered it to his parents with some apprehension. How would they react? He hoped they would accept.

His parents reacted to the invitation with reluctance. They really didn't want to visit the Tramontis. Why would they do something to look as if they approved of the situation? How could they decline when Augustino was so anxious for them to accept the invitation? Besides, Carmella was very curious to see Angelina's home and living conditions.

Meanwhile, Angelina and her sister Mena did whatever was possible to make a good impression on the Rossis. They went to their Aunt Concetta's where their sister Lotti was living. Their Aunt let them borrow some fancy serving dishes, china teacups and saucers, and an elegant coffee urn. The day before the visit they baked biscotti and a ricotta pie. They were as prepared as possible.

On the designated Sunday the Rossi arrived with a somewhat superior attitude and an expensive bottle of wine. Angelina's family welcomed them warmly—the two families doing a quick calculation of each other.

Carmella Rossi felt humiliated to have allowed herself to be put in this position. The home was as she expected—unrefined and plain—one suitable for immigrant boarders. She had to admit the coffee was good and served in china teacups fom an elegant coffee urn. Also, Angelina's brothers were handsome men and her sister Mena was very beautiful. However, there were rumors about her somewhat questionable lifestyle. To be expected from a family of their caliber!

In spite of Carmella's musings, the visit seemed to be going well. Mrs. Tramonti and Augustino's parents had quite a lively conversation in Italian talking about pleasantries and the news of the day. Nothing was mentioned about Angelina's and Augustino's relationship.

Angelina was anxious about this visit. She wanted everything to go well. Even though she was trying not to look obvious, she could see Mrs. Rossi was observing everything in the room The most unanticipated moment came when Mrs. Rossi asked to use the bathroom. Oh no, that conniving witch! Now she would get to see more of the house including the bathroom! The house was in order and clean, but Angelina was sure Mrs. Rossi would examine everything with a jaded eye.

Mrs Rossi emerged from the bathroom which she hadn't used with a smug look on her face. She could see much to her satisfaction, her little trip had caused some anxiety among Angelina's family. These people and Angelina were definitely not up to her standards. As far as she was concerned they were peasants. She didn't know what her husband mean't when he said he would take care of it, but whatever it was, it had better work.

After another half-hour of struggling conversation, the Rossis decided it was time to leave. Thank yous and handshakes were shared. No mention from the Rossis of seeing them again. No return invitaton.

After the Rossis left, the Tramontis looked at each other, rolled their eyes, and gave a sigh of relief. They all had realized Augustino's parents felt they were superior to them—especially Mrs. Rossi. She would be hard to deal with. Mr. Rossi seemed more congenial, but they had a feeling he could not be trusted. However, the visit had gone as well as could be expected.

Augustino was very satisfied with the visit. He would encourage his parents to invite the Tramontis to their home. Now that they had met, he was ready to go ahead with his plans to ask Angelina to marry him. Hopefully they would be engaged by Christmas and married in the Spring. When he informed his parents of his plan, suprisingly they seemed to accept it with no reservations. He wondered why.

Costantino was certain Augustino would stand by Angelina no matter how his parents felt. There could be no road blocks from now on. Everything should run smoothly. It would be a relief to his family to be free of Angelina and her greedy ways and expensive taste for things she could not afford.

He didn't realize before this marriage could take place, they would be confronted by the Rossis with something outrageous!

Thirteen

After the families' visit, the Rossis didn't know what direction they should take. Should they pretend to Augustino they were pleased with the outcome, or just be truthful and let him know they were still strongly against the relationship? They didn't have to wait long for their decision to be made.

Augustino could see only positives in the meeting. He kept asking his parents when they were going to invite Angelina's family to their home. It was now November and he was planning to give Angelina an engagement ring for Christmas. He kept putting more and more pressure on them.

His parents reacted to his pleas with dismay. They would have to tell him how they really felt.

To his surprise, his parents told him they were still not happy with his choice. Angelina seemed like a decent girl, but not of their standing. They could not approve of her as his wife.

Augustino was devastated. He thought everything was going smoothly. This was a terrible shock. No amount of threats or talk of losing his inheritance would stop him from being with Angelina. He would disown them as his parents if they could not accept her.

His parents had never seen Augustino so angry or adamant about anything. Usually he had always given in to their requests. After much consideration, they decided it would do no harm to invite the Tramontis for a Sunday dinner. It would be one last hope for Augustino to realize they didn't fit in with their lifestyle.

Finally, the invitation was delivered by Augustino. Of course, the Tramontis readily accepted. On that day Augustino asked to speak with Costantino and Mrs. Tramonti. He told them of his plan to give Angelina an engagement ring at Christmas so they could be married in the spring.

They were thrilled with the news and offered their blessings. Finally their responsibility for Angelina would be over.

The designated Sunday arrived. Mrs. Rossi was ready to welcome the peasants. She had outdone herself with wonderful food, her best china, linens, fresh flowers and candles. She would hopefully make these people feel as uncomfortable as possible in these surroundings. Augustino would see this. She just wanted to get the dinner over with and not have to bother with them again. Much to her surprise, the tribe arrived on time and seemed very happy and at ease.

After they had gathered around the table and before starting to eat, Angelina's brother, Costantino, stood up. He raised his glass of champagne. He spoke in a proud voice saying, "We are so happy to be celebrating today the future of Angelina and Augustino. They have infomed us of their plans to be engaged at Christmas and married in the spring. Congratulations and best wishes to them."

Everyone but the Rossis raised their glasses and shouted, "Congratulations."

Angelina and Augustino were beaming.

The Rossis were dumbfounded. How and when were all these plans made without their knowledge? How dare Augustino do this to them? They must pretend they knew about it or it would be obvious they had not been respected by their son. They suffered through the rest of the meal hardly knowing what they were eating and having trouble swallowing.

The Tramontis, on the other hand, thought they were celebrating a wonderful occasion. They enjoyed the meal, drank all the champagne, and left in a joyous mood after many thanks. Not wanting to deal with any repercussions right at the moment, Augustino left with them.

Carmella was thoroughly shaken at this turn of events. After taking two aspirins, she had to retire to her bed.

Pasquale Jr. thought to himself—let them go ahead with their plans—get engaged—plan the wedding. They were laughing now. When it was the right time, he would hit them with the news.

Fourteen

After the congratulatory dinner, plans started to be made. Augustino and Angelina went to the Holy Ghost Church on Atwells Ave. to set the wedding date for Saturday, May 18. Angelina's family could not afford an expensive wedding reception. The guest list had to be limited to fifty people. Costantino, Angelina, and their mother went to three different restaurants to get prices on dinners. They were all beyond their means. What were they to do? They could never let the Rossis know of their circumstances. They would be disgraced. They had to come up with the money somehow.

Costantino and his brother, Antonio, were both tile setters. Their younger brother, Giuseppe, was a mason. The least expensive restaurant was charging $5.00 a plate and $50.00 for the wine for a total of $300.00. It would be a hardship, but if each of them donated $100.00, the reception would be paid for. All three agreed and the Modesta Club in Providence was given a deposit and booked for the date. The menu would be the traditional Italian wedding dinner. It would start with salad, then soup, macaroni, chicken, peas, mashed potatoes, and of course the wedding cake and ice cream for dessert. Their sister, Mena, at the moment was dating a man who owned a liquor store, and he offered to sell them the wine for half price. That savings went toward buying the wedding cake. Things were working out.

Philomena's sister, Concetta, was a professional seamstress. She made good money from her wealthy customers who lived on the East Side of Providence. She would sew all three gowns for the wedding. The bride, Mena, the maid of honor, and Lotti, the bridesmaid. She knew where to buy quality material at wholesale prices. The cost of the gowns would be minimal. Yes, things were working out.

At Christmas, as planned, Antonio gave Angelina a beautiful diamond engagement ring. Again, glasses were raised around the dinner table to congratulate the happy couple. The only couple that wasn't happy was the Rossis. Angelina couldn't stop looking at the ring. It was the first thing of any value she had ever owned. It was only the beginning of many expensive possessions she planned to obtain in the future. She wore it with a smug satisfaction.

After the holidays, wedding plans were finalized. The invitations were sent out a month ahead of time.

Much to the brothers' dismay, there was an added expense for the bridal bouquets and a three-piece band. This was getting way beyond their means. They had been tapped to the maximum. However, it was worth it to finally have someone else support Angelina.

Meanwhile, Mr. Rossi had been kept informed of all the wedding plans by Augustino who was anxiously waiting for the day. Much to his father's annoyance, he was so anxious he was having trouble sewing a straight seam at the tailor shop. Two weeks before the wedding, Pasquale Rossi Jr. knew all the wedding preparations were complete. Everything was ready for the special day. Now was the time to execute his plan. He made a phone call to Costantino and asked if he could make a visit to talk with him and Mrs. Tramonti about last-minute plans.

Costantino welcomed his suggestion. He and his mother were pleased he was showing so much interest in the event.

Pasquale Jr. arrived at the designated time on a Sunday afternoon.

He had an air of superiority about him. Costantino noticed he seemed full of himself and wondered why.

After being seated in the living-room, Pasquale Jr. started the conversation. He told them he was very disappointed in them because they hadn't had the decency to talk to him about Angelina's dowry. Every bride was given in marriage along with a dowry. Did they think he was going to overlook that? Since they had not come forward to offer anything, he would expect a dowry of at least $250.00. He felt this was a reasonable price considering his family would have the expense and responsibility of Angelina for the rest of her life. Without a dowry there could be no wedding. To his satisfaction he could see the flash of anger on Costantino's face. Mrs. Tramonti went into a coughing spasm. His plan was working. He knew this was a large amount of money for them. They couldn't afford it. The wedding might not happen.

After the initial shock, Costantino pulled himself together. He would not let this bastard see him squirm. He answered in a very calm matter-of-fact tone telling Mr. Rossi he thought a $200.00 dowry would be sufficient. If this was satisfactory, it would be delivered to his home the day before the wedding.

Mr. Rossi insisted on the $250.00 or there would be no wedding.

Costantino thought this son-of-a-bitch is merciless. He knows we don't have the money. He doesn't need it—he's just doing this to hold up or stop the wedding. Swearing under his breath, Costantino reluctantly shook hands with the bastard to seal the deal—a deal he could not fulfill. Mr. Rossi took his leave swaggering out the door.

Costantino looked at his mother's worried face. What were they going to do? They had used every last penny to pay for the wedding. Their intuition about not being able to trust Mr. Rossi had been correct. Maybe it would be a good thing if Angelina didn't wed into such a devious family. What was going to happen? How could they ever find the means to pay that dowry? Would this wedding be able to take place? Most of all, what would be Angelina's reaction?

Fifteen

After the visit with Mr. Rossi, Costantino was furious. That son-of-a-bitch was putting them against the cross to marry Angelina to his son. His demand made for troubled relations between the two families. Evidently he didn't care and hoped the marriage wouldn't happen. He dreaded having to tell Angelina this latest event. She would probably go into a rage and be inconsolable. He would leave it up to his mother to impart the unpleasant news.

His mother seemed to be numb to the situation. It was as if the facts hadn't yet seeped into her brain. She looked at Costantino with a blank expression. It was going to be difficult for her to talk to Angelina.

When Angelina was finally told Mr. Rossi's threatened request, she didn't cry or carry on. She became belligerent. She cursed Augustino's parents—not surprised they would pull such a stunt at the last minute. If her family could not pay her dowry, she and Augustino would get married quietly by the parish priest in the church rectory. It had been done before by one of her cousins whose parents didn't approve of her fiance. If Augustino had any knowledge of his father's deviousness, he wouldn't hesitate to go along with her plan. His family couldn't stop them from being together.

Costantino consulted with his brothers, Antonio and Giuseppe. They had already donated $100.00 each toward the reception. Their bank accounts were drained. However, if this wedding didn't happen, they would lose all respect in the community. Angelina would be disgraced. There would be all kinds of gossip. The invitations had been sent out, the club was rented, everything was ready to take place in two weeks. What were they to do?

They had to come up with a solution. At this point, Angelina's family felt it would be in her best interest to call off the wedding. What kind of a life would she have living with such conniving people? Of course they knew Angelina would never agree. Remortgaging the house was out of the question. They all had worked too hard to have the home free and clear of any debt. Did they have anything of value to sell? What jewelry Philomena had was worth very little. Giuseppe, the youngest brother was a mason. He owned a very large truck for carrying stones and cement. It must be worth at least $250.00. Maybe he could take out a loan against its value! If this was possible, the agreement would be that all the money given as wedding gifts would be used to pay back the loan. They had to pray enough money would be received at the reception to cover it. It was a chance Giuseppe was willing to take to help out his family and sister.

Giuseppe went to the bank the next morning. He brought the bill of sale showing what he had paid for the truck. Because he had good credit, the bank gave him a loan of $250. 00. If he paid it back in thirty days, there would be no interest. Things seemed to be working out.

When Augustino heard his father had asked for a dowry, he was mortified. He knew Angelina's family didn't have that kind of money. It was his parents' way to stop the wedding. He would never forgive them for this disgusting scheme. Their poor judgement had caused ill-will between the families right from the start. Dowry or not, the marriage would take place. He would see to that and wasted no time in telling his parents this.

His parents pretended to be insulted by his accusations. They tried to convince him they had every right to demand a dowry. Angelina was no exception.

After Giuseppe had secured the loan, Costantino had the satisfaction of calling Mr. Rossi to inform him a dowry of $250.00 would be delivered to his home on the day before the wedding. He could hear the disappointment in Mr. Rossi's voice. It was a glorious moment.

Mr. Rossi was not only disappointed but dumbfounded. How had they been able to come up with this amount of money? There seemed to be nothing to stop these people. There seemed to be no way to stop this marriage. His wife would be upset and get headaches when she realized she had to welcome this low-class girl to live under her roof. She would not make life easy for her. It was the custom when the oldest son married, he automatically lived in the home with his parents. Mr. Rossi and his wife still lived with his parents from the day they were married. The house actually belonged to them—to be inherited upon their passing. So it would be with Augustino and his wife. What a sacrifice this would be!

Angelina was grateful for what her brother Giuseppe had done for her. She would never forget or forgive Augustino's parents for what they had put her family through. She entered this marriage with a vengeance. She would make them pay in every way possible. She also had her conniving ways. They didn't realize who they were dealing with. On the other hand, Angelina had no idea the many prices she would have to pay to get what she wanted.

Sixteen

The day of the wedding arrived bright and sunny. Angelina looked radiant in her satin gown trimmed with lace. A wreath of pink roses on her head held a long silk train embroidered with leaves and roses. Her sister, Mena, as the maid of honor, wore a deep pink taffeta gown. Lotti, the bridesmaid, wore a similar gown of a lighter pink. Both wore a garland of roses in their hair and all three carried a bouguet of pink roses which were Angelina's favorite flower. All decorations for the wedding included roses.

Costantino, looking handsome in a suit and tie, had the honor of escorting his sister down the aisle. While he was doing so, he thought of what sacrifices his family had made to get Angelina to this moment. He hoped it had been worth it. He hoped Angelina would have a happy life with Augustino. His brother, Antonio, was the best man and Giuseppe, an usher. They were also giving Angelina all their support. Everything had been well planned.

The fifty guests who had been invited mostly sat on the bride's side of the church. The Rossis were hesitant to invite friends. They had invited only close relatives who absolutely had to attend. The fewer people to citicize Augustino's choice, the better. When the priest announced them as man and wife, Mrs. Rossi felt a stabbing pain in her chest. A headache was definitely forming.

The reception went very well with lots of eating, drinking, dancing and well wishes. Toward the end the bride and groom quietly left to change their clothes and get ready for the honeymoon. After many kisses and goodbyes Mr. Rossi drove them in his new car to the train station. They were to spend a week in New York. Reservations had been made at the New Yorker Hotel. Neither one of them had ever been to that city, so they were anxiously looking forward to it. Besides the fine dining and drinking, the shows and shopping, the main purpose of the trip was for the couple to get to know each other intimately. Augustino was impatiently waiting for the moment when he could take Angelina in his arms and make love to her.

Angelina had a little idea on what to expect. Her sister, Mena, had given her a quick education on the male anatomy, what would happen, and how to react. After a light dinner in the hotel restaurant, it was time for them to return to their room for the night. Angelina went into the bathroom and changed into a silk nightgown Aunt Concetta had sewn for her. Augustino was waiting in bed for her with open arms. She had never seen such a look of desire on his face. She accepted his tender hugs and kisses with pleasure. Suddenly her nightgown was pulled from her shoulders, exposing her breasts. Augustino was touching them, his hands and lips exploring parts of her body she didn't know existed. Then there was the excruciating pain between her legs. What was happening? Was this love? She didn't have time to be embarrassed. It was so overwhelming she lost all her vanity. When it was over, she was completely exhausted. There had been no pleasure in it for her. She had done her wifely duty and wouldn't have to do it again. It was done once to consecrate the marriage.

When Augustino approached her again the following night she was horrified. Why was he doing this to her again? Did he take pleasure in her pain? Her sister, Mena, had explained to her what would happen, but had left out the part that it would happen more than once. Angelina was devastated. She learned to succumb to Augustino's advances night after night with numbness. She found no pleasure in his carresses and sweet words. After so many nights of his so called "pleasure," the pain became more tolerable with each of his disgusting thrusts into her body. Her sister had warned her not to panic if she saw some blood. This would prove she was a virgin. She hadn't asked how this would happen. Now she knew. Her world had turned from a romantic dream into a horrible nightmare. Was this the price she would have to pay for the rest of her life?

When they returned from their honeymoon, Angelina found the prices became even more demanding and demeaning.

Seventeen

Carmella Rossi was busy preparing her home for the return of the newlyweds from their honeymoon. She wasn't happy about welcoming that peasant into her house. Angelina had brought most of her possessions to the Rossi home prior to the wedding because that was where she would be living in the future. Carmella had taken inventory of her meager belongings—two shabby dresses, some tattered-looking underwear, some small, miscellaneous items, and a worn pair of shoes. This girl came from nothing. She would make sure she earned her better lifestyle.

There were five bedrooms in the house. The master on the first floor was occupied by Carmella's in-laws, Pasquale Sr. and Giovannina Rossi who also owned the home. On the second floor she and her husband had the larger bedroom in the front of the house overlooking the street. Her son, Paolo, had the back bedroom—her daughter, Concetta, one of two middle rooms. She would put Angelina and Augustino in the other middle room so they would be between Concetta and Paolo. Not too much privacy for a newly-married couple!

After an horrendous honeymoon week, Angelina dreaded having to live in the Rossi home. She longed to go back to her family but she knew this was impossible. She had fought for this marriage and now it was done. When they arrived home in late afternoon, Carmella and Pasquale Jr. welcomed them with little emotion—no warm embraces or kisses. Carmella had prepared a light meal of chicken and vegetables. A glass of merlot was held high by all the family including Pasquale Jr.'s sister, Maria Bucci, and her husband, Tony, to celebrate Angelina's and Augustino's new beginning.

After dinner Carmella showed Angelina her bedroom and the family bathroom. Angelina felt very uncomfortable when she realized how close her room was to the ones on each side. There was no privacy. How she wished to be back home in her cozy bed with Mena.

Augustino seemed completely happy with the setup. After all, it was only his brother on one side and his sister on the other.

Angelina hoped Augustino would not want to impose his desires on her that night. It was not to be. She was mortified to think his moans and heavy breathing could be heard in the adjourning rooms. To add to her shame, after he was finished with her, she had to walk the whole length of the hall to get to the bathroom. How could she face anyone the next day?

The next morning Augustino went happily off to work in the tailor shop with his father leaving her to contend with Carmella. The first chore waiting for her was cleaning up after breakfast. Carmella let her know it would be her duty every morning to prepare breakfast and cleanup also. She would show her what they wanted to eat and how to prepare it.

The next chore was the laundry. Carmella instructed her to set a big kettle of water on the stove. The hot water was then brought down in the basement and poured into a large washtub. It was Angelina's job to wash the weeks' laundry using lye soap, rinsing it several times in clean water, wringing each piece, and then hanging everything on a clothesline in the backyard. Angelina never minded washing her own family's clothes. She and her mother and Mena would share the work. She resented having to wash all the Rossi's dirty sheets, towels and underwear.

Angelina was also asked to help prepare the evening meal. Carmella stood at the stove looking over her shoulder giving directions. She made Angelina feel she knew nothing about cooking even though Angelina had prepared many a meal at home. She could feel the hairs on the back of her neck start to tingle with agitation. After dinner Angelina was left with the cleanup—mounds of dishes, pots and pans, the stove and table to wash down, and the floor to sweep.

Exhausted, Angelina climbed into bed longing for sleep only to have Augustino ready for more of his "love making." She lay there numb to his carresses. What had she gotten into? Had she gone from the frying pan into the fire? She was not going to be used like this! She would get her payback. She would get what she wanted or their lives would be miserable!

Mrs. Rossi retired to her bed with a satisfied little smile on her face. Now the peasant had a taste of what her life would be like living here. She wondered how long she would last. She had an even better day in store for Angelina tomorrow!

Eighteen

Angelina woke the next morning more tired than when she went to bed. She had a fitful night's sleep trying to forget her horrible first day in the Rossi home. Now she thought anxiously of what was ahead of her this day.

Carmella Rossi had an even busier day planned for Angelina. Besides making breakfast it was soup day and ironing time. She would make that peasant girl earn her keep. Did she really think she would get to live in such a lovely home and raise her station in life without paying a price?

Angelina presented herself in the kitchen on the dot of seven a.m. to prepare breakfast. Carmella supervised her preparing the bacon to its perfect crispness. The eggs had to be seasoned with just the right amount of milk, salt and pepper, and cooked until they were just the right fluffiness and moisture.

After cleaning up after breakfast, it was time to make the beef soup for supper. Carmella stood at Angelina's shoulder making sure she chopped the celery and carrots to the right size and the beef trimmed and cut to the family's liking.

Angelina could feel herself shaking. Was she afraid of this woman or just shaking from stress? Whatever it was, it wasn't good.

While the soup was simmering on the stove, Angelina was presented with two large baskets of the clothes she had washed the day before to be ironed. This took hours of pressing everything from shirts to tablecloths. After such a long time standing on her feet, her back and legs ached. Her body cried out for rest.

This would not happen because the soup was now ready to be prepared for serving. The noodles were cooked, the soup strained to catch any bones. The escarole she had cleaned and cooked earlier was chopped and added to the soup along with the noodles. Just the right amount of grated cheese was added at the end. After supper-another cleanup.

Angelina was seething inside. How could she defend herself against this horrible woman? She had to survive. She would not be treated like an endentured servant. She had to come up with a plan. After thinking for a while, she knew what she had to do.

That night she finally flopped into bed exhausted, her body aching from head to toe. When Augustino started making so called "love" to her she turned away from him. Augustino was surprised and hurt she would act this way and asked her why she was rejecting him. Angelina told him she was exhausted from all the chores his mother was making her do. If it continued this would be the results—she would never feel rested enough to accept his advances.

Augustino was alarmed to hear this. He had no idea what was happening at home while he was at work. He would have to talk to his mother about letting up on Angelina's chores. The next day he approached his mother and hinted to her in a subtle way if she ever wanted to see a grandchild, she had better take away some of his wife's chores.

Carmella got the message loud and clear. That little peasant girl was someone to contend with. She had used the only ammunition she had very wisely.

When Angelina came down to prepare breakfast the next morning, Carmella gave her a nasty look. It made her realize Augustino must have talked to her. Good! After preparing the meal, the cleanup was shared with Augustino's sister, Concetta. From then on some of the chores were shared. She had somwhat won that score, but she still had Augustino to deal with—no more excuses about being tired. However, Angelina felt she still had the bulk of the work on her shoulders. No one was going to take advantage of her. She had a plan.

The following week Carmella was going to a wedding. Angelina was given the task of ironing the very expensive satin dress Carmella was going to wear. By some coincidence the iron overheated and burned a hole right in the front of the bodice. Angelina apologized profusely. Carmella was devastated. She had to make a quick change of outfits at the last minute. Angelina was never asked to iron anything of value again. This cut way back on the amount of ironing she had to do.

A couple of weeks later it just so happened when Angelina was dusting the living room a very expensive figurine fell and smashed into a million pieces. Angelina apologized profusely. Again Carmella was devastated and decided Angelina would not be allowed to dust the living room any more. This saved Angelina a lot of dusting time.

These accidents seemed to repeat themselves in other ways. Whenever Angelina did the wash, it always seemed one or two expensive garments would be ruined by too much bleach. On some occasions the soup had either too much salt or too much pepper making it almost inedible. On one holiday a piece of expensive silverware was somehow "accidently" lost in the garbage. On that same day, while washing the dishes, Angelina "accidently" broke a fine crystal goblet.

Carmella was beside herself. This peasant girl was driving her crazy. Her headaches were coming more frequently and were more painful. Many times she had to retreat to her room, close the shades, and sleep leaving Angelina in charge. Carmella had to admit her daughter-in-law was a klutz. However, she always apologized profusely when anything went wrong. Carmella didn't know how to handle the situation causing her much stress.

Angelina had been relieved of manyof her chores because of her "inability" to perform them without some mishap. What could they do about it? She couldn't be fired. After all, she was part of the family. Her plan had worked well as far as chores were concerned. Less time with chores made for more time with Augustino. That part of the plan hadn't worked in her favor. The last few mornings she had awakened with terrible nausea. Was she coming down with something, or was Carmella's wish for a grandchild going to come true?

Nineteen

After Angelina kept waking in the morning with nausea for the next two weeks, she came to the conclusion she must be pregnant. If she were coming down with something, she would have had it by now. On her mother's recommendation, she went with her to see the family physician, Dr. Ricci. No one prepared her for the mortifying examination. Lying on a hard table, her private parts were spread open under a bright light for the doctor and all the world to see—being poked with metal instruments that sent shivers up her spine. There must be an easier way to find out if you were pregnant. After this demoralizing experience, the doctor ushered her into his office and confirmed the fact she was about six weeks pregnant. The baby should be born around May. She was happy in a way, but a little fearful as to what may be in store for her

When she arrived home, Augustino was anxiously waiting to hear the verdict. He was overjoyed when told he was going to be a father. He couldn't wait to tell his parents.

Carmella accepted the news, cracked a little smile, and congratulated them. She was happy for her son, but not so happy about the fact her grandchild would carry peasant blood in his or her veins.

Pasquale, Jr. on the other hand was thrilled and shook Augustino's hand in congratulations. He embraced Angelina and told her how happy he was.

Angelina's pregnancy went well. She continued to perform her household duties.

Much to Carmella's concern, Angelina did not gain a lot of weight. Even in the late months of her pregnancy, her belly did not get very large. Was something wrong or had they miscalculated. She hoped it was not going to be a sickly baby—those peasant genes!

Now that Angelina was going to bring an heir to the Rossi family, she felt she should be entitled to some worthy possessions. She hinted to Augustino that now, being in a delicate condition during the cold winter months, a fur coat would definitely help to keep her warm. Augustino promptly took the hint and the next day brought her to Morton's Furs. She purchased a beautiful full-length-black Persian Lamb coat with a mink collar and cuffs.

When she arived home wearing it, Carmella eyed it with envy. Again this peasant girl had wisely used the only ammunition she had to get what she wanted. This was almost too much for Carmella to bear. She quickly retreated to her room with two aspirins and a blinding headache.

As Angelina could feel the weight of her child growing heavier, her legs and feet began to ache as the day wore on. She mentioned this to Augustino and hinted a good strong pair of shoes would really help. Augustino immediately brought her to the Pilgrim Company's shoe department. He wanted her to have the best shoes to support her and his child. She purchased a very expensive-stylish pair of leather pumps. Never had she ever worn such wonderful shoes. They fit her feet like a glove. No wonder the people of means had very few foot problems. She wore them home with pride.

Again Carmella was beside herself to see how manipulative this peasant girl could be. It was almost frightening. She was losing control of her household and her son. Another strong headache was forming along with an upset stomach.

Angelina, accompanied by her sister, Mena, took the trolley downcity for another trip to the Pilgrim Company. The most expensive crib and highchair were ordered to be delivered the following week. She also stocked up on baby clothes, blankets and diapers. Now that she had leverage, they would pay for the best for her and her child.

Along with all the purchases, Carmella's headaches grew increasingly worse. When would this exhorbitant spending end?

In the last months of her pregnancy, Angelina complained to Augustino the mattress on their bed was much too soft to support her back. She needed something firmer.

Augustino was concerned. He wanted the mother of his child to be comfortable. They went to Carrolls Furniture Store on Public Street to purchase a firmer mattress.

While there, Angelina fell in love with the most beautiful bedroom set. It was made of birdseye maple with a fancy headboard, a matching bureau and dressing table. "Oh, Augustino," she said, "I would be so happy sleeping in this wonderful bedroom."

He looked down at his wife's pleading face and her swollen belly below and just couldn't deny her.

The mattress and bedroom set were purchased to be delivered within the week.

Carmella couldn't understand why Angelina was removing hers and Augustino's clothing from the bureau drawers in their bedroom. When she saw a large furniture truck stop in front of their house she wondered why.

Angelina greeted two men from the truck and directed them to her bedroom. They proceded to remove the bedroom furniture and bring it down to the basement.

Carmella couldn't believe this was happening in her home. What was going on? What was this peasant girl up to now?

Then from the truck the men carred a beautiful birdseye maple bureau followed by a dressing table, headboard and a mattress.

Continuing to direct the movers where to place the furniture, Angelina walked past Carmella with a smug smile on her face.

Carmella was not only forming a gigantic headache, but a terrible nausea was overcoming her. She had to quickly swallow three aspirin and a drink of brioche before retiring to her bed for two days.

When it was time for Angelina to deliver, the Rossis were in doubt it was imminent. Angelina had not grown very large. They were sure there had been a miscalculation in time.

On the designated date, Angelina started having labor pains.

Augustino didn't pay too much attention because his mother convinced him if she were ready to deliver, the pains would be so strong, she would be screamng and crying out in agony. She knew from experiencing her own deliveries.

Two hours had gone by with Angelina pacing around the house complaining now the pains were so constant it was hard for her to breathe.

The Rossis just laughed saying it had to get a lot worse before anything was going to happen.

Suddenly, to the Rossis' surprise, Angelina ran into the bathroom. She felt a sudden urge to push. She sat on the toilet. She gave a big push. She could feel the baby coming out between her legs. The pain was excruciating. With one last push the child was born—head first into the toilet bowl!

Augustino and his parents were thunderstruck. He rushed into the bathroom and carried Angelina and the baby onto their bed.

She had given birth to a beautiful, healthy boy.

Now they couldn't do enough for her. Call the midwife to finish the job! She had given them a male heir and they had allowed it to be born in such a terrible manner.

Augustino was angry with his mother for giving them the wrong information. Because of her ignorance his son's birth could have gone terribly wrong. Could he ever forgive her? His wife had suffered needlessly. There would be nothing but the best for her and his son from now on.

Carmella couldn't believe Angelina had given birth so quickly without one scream. She would bear the guilt of this abomination and her son's wrath for the rest of her life. Endless headaches on the horizon!

Angelina lay in bed holding her newborn son. She looked down lovingly at his beautiful sleeping face. In her mind she said to him, "Don't worry my love. They will pay for what they have put us through today. We have the power now. This is only the beginning."

Twenty

Angelina's doctor ordered her to have bed rest for at least a week after the birth of her son. She wallowed in all the attention bestowed on her. It was most gratifying to know she and her son were now the center of activity in the household. She used it well. Her family came to visit bearing gifts and words of encouragement. Her sister, Mena, came every day to help with whatever was needed.

This interruption in her routine upset Carmella to the point of distraction. She didn't like those peasants in and out of her home. Her headaches were becoming unbearable.

Augustino's father, was thrilled to have a grandchild. Pasquale, Sr. was so taken by the little one he couldn't do enough for him or Angelina. Angelina realized this and used it to her advantage.

The infant was a strong, healthy boy with beautiful even features He would grow into a very handsome man. Being a calm baby, he fussed little, nursed regularly, and slept for long hours. He was sleeping through the night in a short time.

According to the Catholic church, a baby had to be baptized almost immediately after birth to remove the original sin from its soul. If anything happened before this, the child would have no chance of going to heaven. Therefore, it was imperative that the boy be baptized within three weeks.

Angelina and Augustino decided to name him Antonio in memory of her father. The godparents were Angelina's sister, Mena, and Augustino's brother, Paolo. Angelina would not be attending the baptism. Mothers were advised by their doctors not to leave the house for at least forty days post partum to give their bodies time to heal. Because babies had to be baptised sooner than forty days, mothers never attended their child's baptisms. Only the father went to the church with the godparents. After the church ceremony, Angelina's family had a reception at their home to celebrate little Antonio.

Carmella was very relieved she didn't have to entertain all those peasants in her home.

Little Antonio flourished and soon developed into a sturdy baby who was doted on by both sides of the family. His father and grandfather especially catered to his every need. By the time he was two years old, another baby was added to the family. He was named Cosimo. This infant was not a robust baby like Antonio. He was very small at birth and quite frail—characteristics that would plague him throughout his life. Because of this, his mother always worried about his health and gave him special attention.

Angelina became pregnant for the third and last time when Cosimo was two years old. She gave birth to a girl they named Etta. She was feisty from day one with a spirit neither one of her brothers possessed. Augustino didn't like the fact being a girl she would put up a fight for what she wanted. Too bad at least one of his sons didn't seem to have that quality.

Family life went along quite normally over the next few years. The children's father and grandfather took care of their every need. Angelina made sure she and her children had the best of everything, clothes, toys, even a new Buick automobile so they would be more comfortable when traveling. Because Angelina had never owned anything of value, she looked upon her children as her possessions. They belonged to HER and no one would ever take them away. God help those that tried! She and her children had now become the core of the family.

Carmella had now relinquished more of her control of the household to Angelina. She was now the center of attention to her son, husband and father-in-law. She demanded, and they couldn't fulfill the demands fast enough.

The winter of 1932 was very severe with freezing temperatures, howling winds and viscious snowstorms. Little Cosimo, being on the frail side, contracted pneumonia. He fought for his life for weeks until gaining the strength to recuperate. Everyone in the family contracted some form of a cold and fever. It was a never-ending winter dominated by illnesses and confinement.

When spring finally arrived the family felt a sense of freedom from the doldrums of the winter. They looked forward to the summer and a new beginning.

Little did they know what a horrible tragedy lay ahead!

Twenty-One

The Rossi family life was good. Augustino and his father did well in the tailor shop so money was plentiful. The children had the best clothes, food, toys, and summers at the shore.

Antonio, at the age of ten, had grown into a sturdy and handsome boy. He was the pride of his parents and grandfather Pasquale. They doted on him and Angelina knew he would be the son who would take care of them in their old age. Her youngest son was small and frail. He didn't possess the strength of character needed to take charge of a situation.

Angelina's brother, Giuseppe, the mason, was building a very intricate stone wall and expressed a desire to bring Antonio with him someday to see how walls were constructed. Stonemasons were highly respected for their knowledge. To learn how to make a stone wall took long hours of on-the-job-training with a good stonemason. It wasn't just a simple task of piling one stone upon the other. They had to know how to prepare the ground, how to place the stones for balance, and make sure the wall had proper drainage so it would last forever. Monetarily it was a very proficient trade. Secretly Giuseppe was hoping Antonio would take an interest and learn the art from him.

With his parents' permission, Antonio agreed to go with Giuseppe. It was a sunny, bright, September day when Giuseppe drove up in his large dump truck to pick up Antonio. His truck was loaded to the top with huge boulders. Some would be used as they were. Others would be cut to fit certain spaces.

They arrived at the construction site. Half the wall had been completed. These rocks were to be used for the top portion. Giuseppe got out of the truck and instructed Antonio to stand to one side in back of the truck and watch the rocks as he dumped them. If the pile got too high, he was to tell Giuseppe to stop dumping there and move forward to the next spot. Antonio was standing behind the truck watching the boulders fall to the ground. As he was told, when the pile got too high, he called to Giuseppe to move ahead.

Suddenly one of the boulders ricocheted off another. As they were falling, a huge one hit Antonio, knocking him to the ground and crushing his body. Giuseppe heard Antonio's scream and rushed to the back of the truck. Half of the boulder was still on Antonio's body. He was screaming in pain. Blood was everywhere. Giuseppe tried to remove the boulder, but it was impossible for him to do it alone. It was a frantic situation.

Finally a car approached and Giuseppe flagged it down.

A young man got out of his car. Between the two of them they were able to roll the boulder off Antonio's body. Antonio was in rough shape and writhing with pain. He had many cuts and bruises, but luckily his head had missed the worst of the blow. He had to get to a hospital immediately.

Giuseppe asked the young man if he could take Antonio to the hospital.

The young man refused saying he couldn't get all that blood in his new car.

Giuseppe had no recourse but to bring Antonio in his huge dump truck still half-full of rocks.

The young man helped Giuseppe lift Antonio, screaming with

pain up into the seat of the truck. Giuseppe was so shaken he drove to the hospital in a state of shock. He would never be able to forgive himself. How could he get the courage to tell Augustino and Angelina this terrible news?

At the hospital the doctors rushed Antonio into the examining room to tend to his injuries.

Meanwhile, Giussepe had to make the horrific call to Augustino at the tailor shop. He would let him break the news to Angelina.

When Angelina heard what happened she felt she was going to faint. What terrible thing had happened to her precious Antonio? Was he going to live? She couldn't bear to think of such a thing. She and Augustino rushed to the hospital.

When they arrived there, Antonio was still being examined. He had been given a sedative for the pain. When he saw his parents he looked at them with a blank stare. He couldn't communicate. He was in a state of shock.

After hours of many tests and x-rays, the doctor in charge came out to the waiting room where Angelina, Augustino and Giuseppe had been anxiously waiting. Angelina was in tears.

The doctor had some good and bad news. Antonio had suffered some bad bruises and would be in pain for quite awhile until everything was healed. There didn't seem to be any internal injuries or bleeding. His head had escaped all real damage. He should recover without any problems. The bad new was his left arm had been completely crushed by the boulder. It was so mangled there was no way of saving it. To prevent further infection and gangrene, the arm would have to be amputated.

A breathless silence hung in the air until the news sank in.

Augustino and Giuseppe put the heads in their hands and wept silently.

Angelina made a tortured scream crying "No, no, no—it can't be true!" She cried uncontrollably until no more tears would come. She thought to herself she wished he had died rather than to go through life so maimed. No one would want him. What kind of a future would he have? The only good thought she had was now she could be sure he would definitely be the one to take care of her and her husband in their old age. What else would there be for him in life? However, in the future, to her dismay, she would find—

Fate had other plans for Antonio!

Twenty-Two

After his horrendous accident, Antonio had to stay in the hospital for three months until his body and what was left of his arm had completly healed. It was a frantic time for the family. Angelina went to the hospital every day. Carmella had to resume most of her duties and manage the household.

Little Cosimo lost his place as Angelina's center of attention. All her concern and attention was now placed on Antonio.

Etta was kind of lost in the shuffle, but having an independent nature, she was able to cope.

When Antonio came home he was doted on by everyone especially his grandfather Pasquale. Tutors were brought in to help Antonio keep up with his schoolwork. A prosthesis was made to fit Antonio's stump. It was very heavy and cumbersome. Antonio tried to wear it, but it was very uncomfortable. It didn't work out.

After an absence of two years, he returned to school. It was a difficult time for him to merge back into the system. He found it hard to keep up with his classes. He made some good friends, but because of his handicap he was also the butt of cruel jokes and hurtful comments. He had to develop a thick skin to survive. He became very adapt in taking care of his physical needs. As he grew older he developed a close group of friends and surprisingly kept up with their many activities.

The relationship between Angelina, Augustino, and her brother Giuseppe remained strained. He had apologized profusely many times and offered to pay for Antonio's medical expenses. Even though Antonio's parents held a deep resentment toward Giuseppe, they did realize they had given their permission for Antonio to go with him that day. It was an accident Giuseppe had no control over. However, their feelings could never be fully resolved.

Giuseppe would carry heavy feelings of guilt for the rest of his life. Every time he saw Antonio the guilt became deeper.

Meanwhile Angelina's demands became even greater. Because of Antonio's accident and the trauma and heartache it had brought into her life, she felt she was due more indulgences. She was very envious of anyone who had more than she, especially her younger sister, Mena. Mena had married well. Her husband was a realtor and was top salesman in his company. She had a gorgeous home on three acres. Everything from the home itself to the interior and furnishings were custom made. When she visited, Angelina would always have a hard time hiding her jealousy.

Her home could never compare with Mena's. She kept making Augustino aware of the fact she was not satisfied with their living conditions. They needed a larger home now that the family was growing.

To satisfy her constant badgering, Augustino purchased three acres of land in the country, promising Angelina he would build a new home there in the future.

As her children grew older, Angelina became even more possessive. She was very aware of who they had as friends especially those of the opposite sex. No one was going to interfere and benefit financially by becoming involved with her children. No one was going to reap the benefits of her struggles and hard work.

Her younger son, Cosimo, became friendly with a girl at school. According to Angelina she came from "the other side of the tracks."

Cosimo made the mistake of bringing her home to visit. Angelina quickly found fault saying she smelled, her clothes were dirty especially her bra that could be seen through her sleeveless dress. She let Cosimo know she disapproved of the relationship. She needn't have worried because Cosimo was not that interested in women. Somehow he felt it was expected of him at his age but his heart was not in it. He really didn't care about having a relationship with anyone.

Etta was a beautiful girl and attracted many young men. Of course Angelina found fault with all of them. None of them were good enough for her daughter. Etta didn't let that stop her from getting involved with whomever she pleased. Somehow her mother always found a way of discouraging them with her sarcastic remarks and pointed questions. After so much of this, Etta started secretly meeting boys and never bringing them home.

At least Angelina didn't have to worry about Antonio getting involved with the opposite sex. Because of his handicap no one would want him except her. He truly belonged to her for life. He would be the chosen one to take care of her and Augustino in their old age. Not to worry.

Then a force named Gloria came along!

Twenty-Three

Gloria Ferri was a very attractive girl with a beautiful face and a figure to match. She was brought up in an upper-middle-class family, the third child in a family of seven. Besides her parents she had three older sisters and three younger brothers. Her father was a hard worker and had provided the family with a subsancial living. Unfortunately, he died very young of a heart attack leaving Gloria and her siblings to fend for themselves.

Gloria was determined to attend college. She was smart, loved learning, and always made the honor roll. While in high school, she worked nights, weekends and summers to save for college. After applying, she was readily accepted at the University of Rhode Island.

Antonio was also attending the same University. Because of his handicap, Antonio was not able to work in the tailor shop with his father. His grandfather, Pasquale, had offered to pay for all four years of college. He wanted to make sure Antonio could make a good living, so he encouraged him to take the business course. Antonio wasn't too interested, but went along with it to please his grandfather. He had always hated school and wasn't a very good student. Because of his accident, he had been set back almost two years in school and could never seem to catch up with his class. The painful questions, remarks and whispers behind his back hadn't helped either. However, he would give it a try.

Antonio and Gloria had the same class in Business English. Antonio admired Gloria from afar. He was impressed by her beauty, her curvaceous figure, and especially her full breasts which pressed firmly against any sweater she wore. Even though he fantasized, he didn't think he would stand a chance with her or any girl for that matter.

Antonio had no idea, but Gloria had noticed him from the first day of class. She thought he was the most handsome man with his aqualine nose, strong jaw and bright blue eyes. His handicap didn't bother her in the least, in fact, it made him more endearing to her. While walking out of class one day, she made it a point to talk to him with the excuse of a question about the next assignment.

He was shocked and pleased she had gone out of her way to speak to him. He answered with a vague response. After they had exchanged a few pleasantries, their conversation just seemed to flow. Words came easily. It was as if they had known each other for a long time.

Gloria was overcome with feeling for him. After their close conversation, she was completely taken by him in every way. She was his if he wanted her.

Antonio couldn't believe how fortunate he was to have this beautiful girl interested in him. He would be cautious however in not hoping for too much. Would her interest go further than just being friends? Over the years he had built up a wall to protect himself from being hurt or disappointed. If Gloria let him down, she was someone who could really destroy his defenses.

Every day after that first encounter, Gloria and Antonio spent every spare moment together. They did their Business English assignments and ate lunch with each other. They seemed to bond with no problem, and basked in the glow of each other's personality.

Antonio couldn't keep his excitement to himself. He would brag to his friends about this beautiful girl who was interested in him.

When Antonio felt Gloria's feelings for him were genuine, he decided it would be safe asking her to dinner.

Gloria was more than happy to accept. It would be wonderful to spend an entire evening with Antonio.

If Antonio wanted to take Gloria to dinner, he would have to ask his father if he could use the family car for the evening. Of course this led to many questions as to why he needed it. When Antonio explained the reason, Augustino could see how excited he was when he talked about Gloria. He was amazed and pleased his son had found someone who could make him so happy. He could certainly trust Antonio to use the car for the evening

Angelina was not happy when she heard the news. Antonio interested in some girl? What girl would be interested in Antonio? She would make a fool of him. He would end up being hurt. Antonio had filled her ears with how beautiful this Gloria was. If she was that beautiful, why would she be interested in Antonio? She must have some agenda. She probably thinks Antonio has money. Just the thought of some other woman riding in her car was disturbing. She would do everything to protect her son from this intruder and discourage the relationship. Antonio was to take care of her in her old age. This girl was upsetting the applecart. She disliked her already. She would make sure this schemer would not get Antonio or any of his money.

Gloria was completely unaware of the fact that, in Angelina's world, she was a force to be reckoned with.

Twenty-Four

Only Angelina's family knew how greedy and demanding she was. To all other people in her world she seemed to be the perfect wife, mother, and the kindest-most-giving person. She was very careful to maintain that persona. When anyone she knew was going through a hard time or illness, she always brought a cooked dish or a dessert to their home. In some cases, depending on the recipients, these visits were done with genuine feelings, but most times they were to maintain her wonderful image not only to herself, but to others. On the way to a wake she could be talking and laughing right up to the door of the funeral home. As soon as she entered, her face could suddenly change to one of complete sorrow and pain. No liquor ever passed her lips—not even a sip of wine, for fear she would lose control and let down her guard. She was the only one in her family to attend mass every Sunday—a true pillar of the church. Such a devout person could be nothing but kind. This was the image she projected.

When Antonio announced he was bringing Gloria home to meet her and Augustino, at that time, to the best of her ability, she would try to welcome this girl and make her feel comfortable. There would be no sign of rejection.

When Gloria met Angelina she did feel welcome, but also felt there was a certain cold reserveness about her She seemed like someone you could never quite get close to. However, maybe it was her imagination.

Antonio's father, Augustino, seemed like a warmer person. He seemed genuinely happy to meet her.

Over dessert and coffee Angelina had the opportunity to study this girl and ask a few pertinent questions. She was, as Antonio had told her, a beautiful girl, well spoken, and impeccably dressed. There didn't seem to be anything she could find wrong. This made her even more suspicious. Why would this girl be attracted to her son? She must have some agenda. As Antonio had mentioned previously, Gloria, on being questioned, confirmed the fact that she too, as Angelina, had lost her father at a young age. Angelina had no sympathy for her. It couldn't compare with what she had to go through. She didn't have to work hard and live with boarders. A streak of jealousy arose in her. She resented this girl for upsetting her future plans with Antonio. Hopefully she could make him see what a mistake he was making.

Gloria felt good about her visit to Antonio's home. It seemed she had made a favorable impression on his parents, although she had some reservations about his mother. Angelina had asked a lot of personal questions about her family. She had also slipped in a few remarks about how much she relied on Antonio to take care of her and her husband in their old age. Gloria didn't know if she should resent these remarks or disregard them even though she thought they were uncalled for.

Antonio and Gloria were deeply in love. Despite Angelina' constant badgering Antonio about not getting too involved and trying to find some made-up flaw in Gloria's character to warn him about, their love persevered through four years of college. After graduation, Gloria was employed at The Newton Press as an editor, and Antonio found work at Princeton Associates as an accountant. Now they were ready to move on. Marriage shouldn't be too far in the future.

All the years they had been together their lovemaking had become intense but just short of "going all the way." Following the rules of morality and the Catholic church, this was something a decent girl never did before marriage. Men respected this. Self control and the fear of pregnancy bringing disgrace on one's family also played a large part in relationships in that era.

Gloria was looking forward with anticipation to the day she and Antonio would finally marry. Whenever she mentioned it to him he seemed to change the subject. He couldn't be pinned down. She wondered if he was losing interest in her. Why was he so noncommital? They both had good jobs and could support themselves. There didn't seem to be anything now to prevent them from getting married.

Over the years Angelina had seemed to be so supportive of Gloria and their relationship. She seemed to accept her in every way, meeting her family, having Gloria for dinner every Sunday, and even exchanging gifts on birthdays and Christmas. What Gloria didn't realize in her innocence was the kind of a scheming, conniving woman she was up against. Beneath this friendly facade, the real Angelina was constantly warning her son about the pitfalls of marriage, and filling him with guilt by letting him know how much his parents were depending on him to take care of them in their old age. If he married, his loyalty to her would be broken.

Antonio was torn between wanting to be with Gloria but not disappointing his mother. His mother had a great influence over him. He remembered how she had taken care of him after his accident, her complete devotion to his every need. They had a history. How could he disappoint her? He had to come to grips with the situation. He loved Gloria very much, but who should come first in his life? It was a decision that would have to be made. One of them was going to be hurt.

Twenty-Five

Antonio kept struggling with his decision. Should he disappoint his mother or Gloria?

Gloria, meanwhile, was getting more impatient. What or who was his problem? After three months of Antonio vascilating, Gloria finally gave him an ultimatum. Either he made a decision in her favor, or the relationship was over. There would be no more waste of her time. She must get on with her life. She wanted a family.

This threat was enough to jolt Antonio from his indecision. He couldn't take a chance Gloria would leave him. He didn't have to, but he talked it over with his parents. Much to his mother's annoyance, her husband encouraged Antonio to make the move toward marriage. Gloria was a wonderful girl, beautiful, smart, and had been faithful to him for almost five years. There should be no hesitation.

When Angelina tried to give one more reason why Antonio should not marry Gloria, Augustino told her to be quiet and not interfere with the young couple.

She resented her husband for not agreeing with her and felt cast aside. This girl was already causing trouble between them. It upset her greatly to think Gloria would be getting a diamond engagement ring. If it was up to her, she would do everything in her power to see this girl never got anything of value in the future.

After talking with his parents, Antonio quickly went to see Gloria. He wanted to mend the relationship. He told her not to worry; they would be engaged soon.

This pleased her, but overshadowed what in her mind should have been a more spontaneous surprise. She had always dreamed of the lover getting down on one knee and unexpectedly whipping out a small velvet box revealing a sparkling diamond ring. Then the proposal! Oh well, maybe she was too much of a dreamer.

To diminish the surprise even more, he asked her what kind of a diamond she would like. She told him a plain, round diamond with no embellishments around it would be fine. She didn't care about anything fancy or very large to compete with other engaged girls. Hopefully, at least the day Antonio would present her with the ring would be a surprise.

However, a month later Antonio announced he had the ring and would be coming that evening. Gloria was anticipating his visit all day. When Antonio finally arrived, he didn't seem in any hurry to give her the ring. He made small talk as if it were just another usual evening. For Gloria, knowing he had it in his possession and not coming forward with it was very frustrating. She almost wanted to reach into his pocket and put it on herself. Why was he hesitating? Was he holding off until the last minute almost making her beg for it?

When he finally slipped it on her finger she was happy, but there was no proposal, and much of the joy and excitement of the moment had been diminished. It was a lovely diamond just as she had described, but the manner in which it had been presented left much to be desired. How unromantic!

A few days after the engagement, Antonio brought Gloria to his home to receive congratulations from his family. When they arrived no one was in sight. Angelina had heard their car coming in the driveway and quickly ran down to the basement, pretending she was doing laundry. She didn't want Gloria to think she was anxiously waiting to congratulate her. She would let them wait awhile before going upstairs. It would be painful enough for her even then. When she finally composed herself, she went upstairs and feigned surprise at seeing them, pretending she didn't know they had arrived. In a cool, almost disapproving manner, she took Gloria's hand, looked at the ring, and almost choked on her words of congratulation. She then quickly left the room with the excuse of more chores to do. It killed her to see Gloria get anything of value—especially anything their money had to pay for.

Gloria could feel the resentment and was puzzled at Angelina's behavior.

Later, the rest of the family appeared from wherever they had been to offer their congratulations. Antonio's sister, Etta, congratulated Gloria and was happy to see her own engagement ring was much larger. As long as whatever she had was bigger or better than anything Gloria had, it would be easy to deal with.

Now that they were finally engaged, Gloria wondered if setting the wedding date would be just as tedious a struggle making Antonio commit.

Even though Angelina was not happy with the situation, she could never let her true feelings be known. She had to keep up appearances as the kind, caring person who could never do any harm. The pillar of the family. She would plan a small engagement party to make it seem she was happy and fine with everything. This would be only the first of many acts that would seem to be for but were really against the upcoming marriage—a marriage she hoped wasn't going to happen.

Twenty-Six

After their engagement, Gloria was anxious to set a wedding date. However, of course, Angelina was looking for as many deterrents to wedding plans as possible. Her daughter, Etta, had recently become engaged also to a man who was a very sucessful contractor. Etta had paid no attention to her mother's warning about the character of this young man. Etta had made up her mind, and no one could deter her from the decision to marry him. Because they had set their wedding date for the coming year, it served as a good excuse to postpone Antonio and Gloria's wedding to the following year.

Gloria was disappointed, but accepted it graciously. She even was a bridesmade in Etta's wedding.

The following year when Gloria's wedding plans were starting to take shape, Angelina decided it was time to pay a visit to Gloria's mother. She and her husband arrived on the designated day. Angelina was impressed by the lovely home where Gloria had grown up. Her feelings of resentment again came to the surface. She tried to impress Gloria's mother by talking about all her own accomplishments— sewing, quilting, embroidery, knitting, cooking, and on and on.

In turn, Gloria's mother was duly impressed. She thought Angelina was a wonderful person who wished only the best for the newlyweds.

After Angelina was done bragging, she brought up the subject of the upcoming wedding. The three parents discussed the wedding plans as though Gloria and Antonio were not there. Angelina made it clear the wedding could not take place on Saturday as Gloria had planned. Saturday was the busiest day in the tailor shop and if they closed, they would lose money. It would have to be on a Monday. On Monday most of Gloria's friends and co-workers would find it hard to get the day off to attend a wedding. However, far be it for Gloria to feel guilty about making her in-laws lose money. She had no choice—it would have to be Monday. Also the in-laws felt the upcoming summer when Gloria wanted to have the wedding on her birthday was too soon for them to prepare. It would be better in the fall. What else were they going to change about her wedding day? Was it hers or theirs?

Before the wedding, Angelina, again to keep up her image of the wonderful mother and mother-in-law to be, planned a surprise bridal shower for Gloria at her home. This would give her a chance to show off all her talents fom the knitted afghan on the sofa to the embroidered pictures on the wall and her home-made desserts.

Gloria's mother and the in-laws had decided they would go half on the expense of the reception. This, unfortunately gave Angelina some input in the plans which she readily took advantage of. She demanded she and her husband's names be on the wedding invitation along with Gloria's mother. Gloria knew this wasn't the proper way for an invitaton to be worded Only her mother's name should appear on the invitation as the person who was giving her in marriage. Her friends and associates would think she didn't know the correct procedure. But to keep the peace, she went along with it.

Gloria wanted to make her wedding reception a little different from the norm. She decided she would go with the latest trend of having a buffet instead of the usual Italian sit-down dinner.

Angelina thought this was ridiculous. Because she was paying half the bill, it gave her the right to call the restaurant and tell them they had changed their minds. They no longer wanted a buffet, but would like the platters of food passed among the seated guests. No one should have to stand in line to get food.

On the day of the reception Gloria was terribly upset to see waiters bringing platters of cold cuts and salads to the tables instead of having a buffet table tastefuly arranged with flowers and candles as she had ordered. It completely changed the atmosphere she had wanted to portray. She didn't know how this mistake had happened or who was responsible. It was too late now to do anything about it. She bit her lip and tried to hide her disappointment. This, she was to find out, was just the beginning of many puzzling interferences she would have to contend with in the future.

Gloria and Antonio started looking for apartments six months before the wedding. They found a beautiful one in a good neighborhood for the price they could afford. They put a down payment to hold it until they could move in.

When Antonio's father heard about it, he disapproved of what they had done. He didn't want them paying rent. They would be better off buying a house and building up equity.

This was something Gloria was not ready for. She would be happy for now living in that cozy little apartment.

However, once Antonio heard of the proposal, there was no holding him back. He and his parents started the search for a house the newlweds could buy. Antonio and his parents found a small bungalow in Johnston they felt would be the perfect fit for the newlyweds. When Antonio told Gloria about it she became adament. She was angry about the fact he and his parents went looking for a house for her to live in. She didn't appreciate their interference. If they thought it was such a good idea for them to buy a house, she would be the one to pick it out.

After more searching, Gloria found a small, newly-built raised ranch nearer to where she worked and within their price range. To make the down payment Gloria put a thousand dollars of her money,

Antonio put a thousand, and the remaining two thousand they borrowed from Angelina's brother Giuseppe. Angelina and Augustino would not give them any money for the down payment because they were afraid, being the parents, they would not get paid back. Angelina wanted none of her money invested in anything Gloria would own. She was resentful her son would be living on the other side of the city and not nearer to where the house she had picked was located. She was also furious to think Gloria would be moving into her own home right after the honeymoon. She hated the thought of that girl owning anything of value.

Augustino could see the fury building in Angelina. He quickly calmed her down. He told her this had all been part of a plan. Gloria thought she was buying a house. She would be paying the mortgage and insurance on a house she thought she owned. Not to worry—Angelina would be relieved when he explained his plan to her.

Twenty-Seven

To save himself from Angelina's wrath and jealousy about Gloria and Antonio buying their own home, Augustino quickly sat her down to explain his plan. He would tell the newlyweds-to-be they didn't have enough equity to purchase the house on their own Therefore, he and Angelina would have to purchase it for them. He and Angelina's names would be on the deed as the owners. As soon as they came back from their honeymoon they would tell them they would deed the house over to them. Of course they had no intention of doing this. Hopefully Gloria would forget about it also. It would be their way of aquiring a home without paying for it. They knew how difficult Antonio was to live with. He would go into dark moods and be irritable over litle mishaps. They had their doubts this mariage would last. If it didn't, they would give Gloria her deposit back and the house would belong to them. It wouldn't be divided in half. Their son would be protected.

Gloria wasn't very comfortable with this arrangement, but Antonio was convinced this was the only way they could buy the house. As soon as they came back from the honeymoon, Gloria was anxious to have the deed put in their name. At this point she was earning more than Antonio and was very consciencious about paying the bills, especially the mortgage, taxes and insurance. Months went by and there was no attempt by the in-laws to turn the deed over to them. She kept mentioning her concern to Antonio, but he never seemed worried about it. After almost a year had gone by with no sign of the deed being transferred, Gloria decided it would be up to her to approach the subject.

Every Sunday Gloria and Antonio were expected to go to his parents' house for dinner. If they didn't, Angelina would have made Antonio feel guilty because he would be neglecting her. It was easier just to go and avoid the backlash. These Sunday dinners meant a lot to Angelina. It gave her something to look forward to every week. It was her entertainment. It also made her feel she still had some control.

On one of these Sundays Gloria brought up the subject of the deed. She reminded them of their promise to transfer the deed to them when they returned from their honeymoon. It was almost a year and nothing had been done. Had they forgotten?

Angelina and Augustino looked outraged. They acted as if they had been wrongfuly accused of doing something dishonest. How dare she? They quickly assured her it had just been overlooked. They would attend to it as soon as possible. They both looked so disappointed and downcast as if they had been deeply wounded by this accusation. Antonio could see how much Gloria had upset his parents. This definitely put Gloria in a bad light in his eyes. Gloria had been turned into the wrong doer. This was only the beginning of many situations where Gloria looked like a troublemaker when she was only standing up for her rights.

Angelina had to give that little minx credit for fighting for what was hers. Evidently she wasn't someone who could be fooled easily. They would have to transfer the deed as soon as possible. They couldn't look dishonest or pretend forgetfulness any longer. There was only one good thing that had come from this. It made Gloria look like a troublemaker.

Twenty-Eight

Antonio's sister, Etta, married Felix Costanza a year before Angelina and Antonio's marriage. She had a fabulous wedding on the third Saturday in April. She wouldn't settle for any other day in the week no matter how much money her father lost in the tailor shop. The Rossis spared no expense in making sure Etta got everything she wished for. The newlyweds spent one year living in an apartment while Etta designed the home that was being built for them to move into when it was completed. It was a beautiful four bedroom two bath ranch with all the amenities on an acre of land, all paid for by the Rossis. Angelina had to make sure her daughter had the best of everything—more than anyone else, especially Gloria.

Meanwhile, Angelina was still waiting for Augustino to begin planning for her house on the three acres of land he had purchased ten years ago. The area had built up somewhat over the years and wasn't as countryish as it used to be. She would always picture the house in her mind. It would be a large white colonial with pillars in the front—very stately looking. A house worthy of her presence.

Two years after Etta's marriage, Augustino's mother, Giovanina, had a stroke. Being in her eighties, she didn't have the stamina to rehabilitate herself. After a long struggle, she succumbed to her illness and passed away that winter just before the holidays. Ironically, it was Angelina who held her hand until she took her last breath. A purple wreath was placed on the front door to let people know of a death in the family. Her body in a rosewood casket was laid out in the parlor for ten days. Mourners could come to express their condolences any time of the day or evening. Someone from the family had to sit with the body at all times. It was a long, tedious, and very depressing rite. When it was over, it left a pall over the household for the rest of the winter.

Now that Pasquale had lost his precious Giovanina, and was alone, he decided it was time to make some arrangements for the future. He had been very generous with Angelina and Augustino up to now. He had paid for all the household expenses, the many upgrades Angelina had wanted, and years of taxes and insurance on the property. He had also been very generous with the children, paying for their clothes, summer vacations at the shore with Angelina, and for Augustino's many new cars, plus the three acres of land in the country. He also paid Augustino a generous salary in the tailor shop.

Now that he could make decisions on his own, he let his plans be known to his family. He would be leaving the house, business, the three acres and any other assets or money to Augustino. However, he was very adamant that everyone understand he wanted the stores that housed the tailor shop left to his grandson, Antonio. Because of his handicap, he wanted to make sure Antonio never had to worry about having enough money to live. He also took out an insurance policy for Antonio that would pay him so much a month after he turned thirty years old. He made out a will stating these facts and gave a copy to Antonio and Augustino.

Angelina was beside herself with these arrangements. She wanted ALL of it. How dare he leave those stores to Antonio? It made her physically ill to think someday Gloria might own that property. This could never happen. She would find a way to make sure it never did.

Meanwhile, Gloria and Etta were busy having babies. Etta had a boy she named Domenic. Six months later Gloria gave birth to a boy she and Antonio named Antonio, Jr.

Angelina became very possessive of Etta's son. She demanded Etta and her husband and the baby stay with her for a little while after Etta was released from the hospital to make sure the baby was well taken care of. Their visit lasted almost a year. Felix finally became impatient living in someone else's house and insisted they return home. However, little Domenic became a constant visitor at Angelina's because Etta couldn't keep him on any kind of a schedule. He was used to being fully entertained at grandma's by being passed from arm to arm between Angelina, Augustino and Pasquale.

Gloria was criticized and given snide remarks for keeping her son on a strict eating and sleeping schedule. When she and Antonio couldn't visit Angelina on a Sunday at the time she preferred because they had to wait until the baby woke up from his nap, she would be furious. She was positive it was done on purpose to get her upset. Gloria would be greeted with sarcastic remarks about getting there when it was time to go home. Gloria tried hard not to feel guilty.

Etta had another child when little Domenic was three years old. She named her Jessica. This child was also taken over by Angelina. It was evident Angelina preferred these two grandchildren and looked upon them as her own. Her daughter was more than happy to relinquish the responsibility to her mother. It was much less work for her.

Gloria had two more children, each two years apart, a boy named Roberto and a girl named Lisa. Angelina was upset, because now Gloria had one more child than her daughter. She knew her daughter wouldn't have any more because she couldn't handle the two she had. Just because Gloria had one more child, didn't mean they would get more than the other two. She would make sure of that.

Even though she could see the favoritism toward Etta's children, Gloria tried to keep the relationship with her in-laws compatable. She decided to invite them to dinner on a Sunday afternoon.

Angelina felt Gloria was trying to usurp her position as the the one who made Sunday dinner.

Gloria was pleased when they accepted and was excited, planning what she would serve.

Meanwhile, Angelina was plotting what she would do to spoil the afternoon. She would make it so miserable Gloria would never ask them again.

Twenty-Nine

Gloria was grateful her in-laws had accepted her dinner invitation, but she felt quite anxious about the situation. She knew how much she almost hated to see her children's birthdays arrive because it meant a dreaded visit from the in-laws. Her mother-in-law considered herself a wonderful baker. Gloria didn't have much luck with even a cake mix. She would feel intimated when her mother-in-law would examine her birthday cakes with a disapproving eye. Then she would pointedly ask for the recipe forcing Gloria to admit it was just a cake mix. The birthdays had become a night of dread and anxiety. In those times, ordering a cake on your child's birthday was considered being lazy and an admission of complete failure as a good mother. It was to be avoided at all costs.

However, she hoped this dinner would be a little different, because she had more confidence in herself as a cook than a baker. She had set the date for the following Sunday afternoon at one p.m. She would serve one of her best recipes, stuffed chicken breasts with gravy, oven roasted potatoes smothered in sweet peas, fresh steamed broccoli sauteed in olive oil and lemon, roasted red peppers, crispy slices of Italian bread, and for dessert, coffee and chocolate cream pie with whipped cream. She set the dining room table with her best china, linens, candles at both ends, and a centerpiece of flowers from her garden. When the day arrived, everything was done on time, the house was spotless, and the table looked beautiful.

Meanwhile, Angelina was playing out her little scheme. At noontime she prepared a meal for Augustino. Since he didn't know what time they were to have dinner at Gloria's, he was hungry and ate everything on his plate. She had no intention of arriving at Angelina's at one-o-clock as expected. She knew the worst experience for a cook was to have the guests arrive late for dinner. The food would start to turn cold and have to be reheated once or twice making it dried out and unappetizing. She would let Gloria wait until almost two-o-clock.

At one-thirty Gloria began to wonder what had happened to her guests. The chicken was still ok even though it wasn't as warm as it should be, but the potatoes had become soft and lost their crispness. By the time they arrived at two-o-clock she was quite annoyed, but didn't let them be aware of it. No excuses were made for their lateness.

When they were finally seated at the table, Angelina had to admit the food looked very appealing. Gloria had really outdone herself. She took a bite-size portion of everything, and then told Gloria Augustino would not be eating much since he had a good meal at noon. Gloria wondered why he would do that knowing he was coming here at one o'clock—or did he? Knowing Angelina, Gloria surmised she was proably so jealous she didn't want Augustino to eat much of her food, fearing he might find it better than hers and even give her a compliment. Another one of her manipulations. To add to the already uncomfortable situation, Angelina "accidentally" knocked over her glass of red wine causing it to spill in the brocolli, the bread, and all over the tablecloth. Gloria tried not to become upset and assured Angelina everything was fine. She assured her the brocolli's flavor would be enhanced by a taste of wine, there was nothing better than Italian bread dipped in wine, and the tablecloth could be washed. This bitch wasn't going to get to her!

After a short forty-five minutes of her guests barely touching their food, Angelina announced they would have to leave shortly because Augustino's father wasn't feeling well and they had to check on him. They wouldn't have time for dessert.

At this point Gloria was glad to see them go. She should have known better than to invite them. Angelina had pulled another one of her stunts. It was getting more difficult to have a civil relationship with this devicive woman.

Angelina left feeling triumphant. Her plan had gone well. If Gloria wasn't a glutton for punishment, she wouldn't invite them again.

She didn't realize what a bigger challenge awaited her and it didn't involve Gloria!

Thirty

Cosimo had never become involved with another girl since Marie, the one his mother didn't approve of because she came from "the other side of the tracks." After high school he joined the Navy. Angelina was hysterical worrying about her son being sent away and out of her control. Once when he came home on leave, he became ill with a very bad cold. When his leave was over and he had to return to base, she contacted his commanding officer and begged him to let him stay home until he was well. Being so sick, he couldn't possibly travel. The officer kindly assured her the Navy was perfectly capable of taking care of him. She had to release him with a tearful goodbye. He served two years during World War II, didn't see any real action, and after being honorably discharged, came home and settled into a mundane existence.

He found a job as a sales clerk in the men's department in Merchants Exchange, a large department store in the city. He soon was promoted to manager. He liked his job and enjoyed helping men pick out their clothes. He had an eye for fashion and was a smart dresser. His one passion was cars. He bought a new car every two years and kept it in pristine condition. They always had to be top of the line.

He had one close friend, a buddy he grew up with who was

married and had four children. He had no social life. At thirty years old his life was comfortable, unstressful, but there was definitely something missing.

Sylvia was nineteen years old and very independent for her age. She also worked at Merchants Exchange in the cosmetics department. She was quite attractive with even features, long auburn hair, hazel eyes and a well proportioned figure. Working with cosmetics, she knew how to apply her makeup to bring out her best features. She and Cosimo would exchange pleasantries on their way to lunch. Eventually they ended up lunching together and having deep conversations. She found herself falling in love with this gentle man. He was also handsome with his blond hair and piercing blue eyes. Their relationship grew stronger. They started meeting after work and going out for dinner. Cosimo felt very comfortable and at ease with Sylvia. He almost started to believe he could have an intimate relationship with her. She was so positive and enthusiastic about everything, it made him feel anything was possible.

After almost two years into their relationship and vowing love for each other, Sylvia wanted to get married. This was something Cosimo had always feared would happen. He tried to convince himself it might work because he did feel a certain love for Sylvia. Marriage would also bring normalcy to his life.

About six months previously he had, against his better judgement, brought Sylvia home to meet his parents. Angelina was surprised. She figured Cosimo was going to be a bachelor. He was thirty years old and didn't seem interested in marriage. Maybe he had decided he was going to be the chosen one to take care of her in her old age. What did this Sylvia have to convince him to take the step? She hadn't been impressed with her. She was too young for Cosimo and didn't seem mature enough at nineteen for marriage. Also, she was Swedish and not Italian. The worst drawback of all was she was a mechanic. Her hobby was working on cars. She loved being under the hood tinkering around. She would come to visit and sit at the dinner table smelling of grease and oil. What was he thinking? She didn't fit in at all. He must have lost his mind.

Cosimo knew his mother and sister, Etta, didn't approve of Sylvia. She didn't fit their mold. Doubts if he was doing the right thing by marrying her would creep into his mind when he was not with her, and he would get one of his painful headaches. When he was with her, she made their future look so wonderful, he actually felt it would be.

The wedding date was set. Angelina refused to give her a bridal shower. She just invited Sylvia's parents and grandmother for an evening of pizza and coffee. Cosimo couldn't be pesent because he was confined to his bed with a blinding headache.

Sylvia's parents reciprocated by inviting all the Rossis for drinks and hors' doeuves. Etta couldn't finish her drink of Johnny Walker because there was a bug in the glass. The evening became dull and boring—conversation strained. It was obvious the Rossis weren't making an effort to be congenial. Gloria felt badly for Sylvia's family because she knew they felt rejection.

The wedding took place in the evening at Sylvia's church. It was a very short and simple ceremony. Cosimo was completely overwhelmed and almost backed out at the last minute. Was he doing the right thing? Was he being fair to Sylvia? His headaches had become more and more debilitating. Being a shy person, on the wedding day he didn't want to take any pictures. He hated being on display with everyone staring at them while being photographed. At Sylvia's urging he agreed to pose for two pictures in front of the altar. It had become a nightmare.

Angelina and Augustino were upset over the marriage, but more so over the couple's living arragements. They had offered them their home to live with them, rent free, and a hot meal to come home to every day after a day's work. Sylvia refused the offer and found a cozy three-room apartment on the other side of the city. The Rossis were completly insulted and disliked Sylvia even more. When they vented their disappointment to Gloria about this, she tried to make them understand how a newly-married couple wanted to be alone and have their privacy. Coming home to a hot meal wasn't that important. She couldn't change their feelings.

The marriage was going well. It seemed to bring Cosimo out of his shell. He was more sociable and seemed happier than he had ever been. He was a new person. They frequently came to visit Gloria and Antonio on Saturday nights making Gloria and Sylvia close friends and confidantes.

Angelina and Etta made themselves aware of everything going on in Cosimo's marriage. They couldn't believe it was working out. When they were in Sylvia's company, they would find fault with any little thing she might say or do they didn't approve of and bring it to Cosimo's attention. Most of all they found it disgusting she worked on cars, and came to supper in her work clothes smelling of the garage. When they found out Cosimo had bought a new car and was going to let Sylvia pick it up at the dealers and drive it home, they pounced on him as if he had committed a murder. How could he allow her to have such a privilege?

Sylvia started visiting Gloria alone in the afternoons. Gloria was always home because she had small children and welcomed the company. One afternoon Sylvia started to confide in her about her marriage problems.

What she told Gloria was most disturbing.

Thirty-One

Gloria and Sylvia became quite close after Sylvia and Cosimo were married. Sylvia took an interest in Gloria's children, and brought them out to the garage and explained all the different parts of an engine to them. The children in turn found Sylvia very interesting and fun to be with. This is why when Sylvia confided in Gloria about the problems in her marriage, it came as a surprise.

According to Sylvia, their marriage was in trouble from almost day one. Cosimo was petrified Sylvia would become pregnant. Even though she assured him she was on the pill, he still took precautions to make sure nothing happened. She was lucky if they were intimate once a month. She was very young and had strong sexual desires. This kind of a life would not be satisfying to her. She loved Cosimo very much and wanted the marriage to work. She had demanded he see a psychiatrist to help him with this problem. Hopefully it would save their relationship.

Gloria sympathized with Sylvia and hoped things would work out for them. She had become fond of Sylvia and would hate to see the marriage fail. She wished her well and asked her to keep her informed of any progress.

Over the next weeks Sylvia continued to visit Gloria and informed her Cosimo was going to see a psychiatrist. What bothered her was Angelina had the nerve to call the doctor to find out what he had talked about. Of course the doctor had infomed her there was a patient-doctor confidentialty law, and he could tell her nothing. However, he did say over-possessive mothers were worse than mothers who were almost neglectful of their children. They smothered them and made them dependent.

Hoping to get her opinion, Angelina told Gloria this. She couldn't believe the doctor had talked to her in such a manner.

Gloria told her she should never have called the doctor. There was a patient-doctor confidentialy agreement. They could never release any information to anyone including mothers. Gloria also silently hoped what the doctor had told her about smothering mothers would change her possessive qualities to some degree. Hoping for that was like hoping for the sun to fall out of the sky.

Sylvia, naively thinking she could trust Angelina with her marital problems, made the mistake of confiding in her. She told her Cosimo was going to a psychiatrist for help. Angelina agreed with her it was a good thing he was going for help. However, when she was alone with Cosimo she told him he didn't need a psychiastrist. There was nothing wrong with him. He just took after his Uncle Tony who wanted to become a priest.

Cosimo innocently relayed this back to Sylvia.

Realizing Angelina had betrayed her trust, she became furious. She went to see Gloria to express her frustrations.

This was the end for Sylvia. She could not see herself living this kind of life and having to deal with such conniving people.

Cosimo reluctantly told his family his marriage was over. Angelina and Etta expressed regrets but were smugly satisfied. They had been hoping for this all along. They started criticising Sylvia, blaming her for the breakup. Not wanting to hear anything derogatory about Sylvia, he stopped them immediately. In no way was this her fault.

Sylvia was heartbroken and very disappointed the marriage hadn't lasted for even ten months. She realized Cosimo had done everything in his power to make it work, but there were problems that were difficult to overcome. His mother was one of his biggest difficulties.

Sylvia asked one last thing of Cosimo before parting ways. She begged him not to go back and live at home again. He was in his thirties and should have a place of his own where he could be independent and away from his parents' control.

When Angelina found out about what he was planning to do, she accused Sylvia of wanting to throw her son "out on the street." She would never let this happen. She immediately redecorated the largest bedroom in her house with new wallpaper, carpeting, bedding and curtains. She showed Cosimo what a wonderful room he would be coming home to, and all the work they had done to make him happy. The spell was cast. He returned home, never to leave until his dying day, leading a life of depression and blinding headaches.

Angelina didn't realize how her plans for Cosimo would backfire on her someday.

Thirty-Two

Etta, Angelina's daughter had married well. Her husband was a very successful in the costruction business. She lived in a lovely home she had designed herself and built to her satisfaction. All the furnishings had been hand picked and were of the best quality. In the backyard was a beautiful inground pool with all the amenities surrounding it, a rarity in the sixties. It looked like it belonged in Hollywood. Etta's daughter and son had been mostly taken care of by her mother, Angelina, relieving her of many motherly duties.

In spite of all the pluses in her life, Etta was not happy. Even though she realized she had much more than anyone else in the family including her sister-in-law Gloria, it didn't take away her feeling of disatisfaction. Her husband was very controlling and possessive; so was her mother. She felt suffocated between the two of them. Her husband wanted to spend weekends together, but her mother made her feel guilty if she didn't go there every Sunday to have dinner. She didn't know how to please both of them. This gave her much anxiety. She wanted to break away and have some life of her own, but didn't have the strength mentally or physically to do it.

Her anxiety turned into anger and then emerged as a phobia. She became a recluse, not going anywhere for fear of contacting some terrible illness. No one was allowed in the house including her children's friends. No windows could be opened for fear of germs in the air. The pool became out of bounds because it would be contaminated by people swimming in it. Her phobia was also a way out of having to go to her mother's house. It proved to Angelina she couldn't go there because she couldn't go anywhere else. It relieved her of any guilt she had felt about this matter.

Angelina was heartbroken over Etta's condition. She blamed her son-in-law for driving her into this state of mind.

Etta went to counselors and psychiatrists but nothing seemed to help. She would call Gloria and talk to her on the phone for hours looking for some consolation. Gloria would listen to her fears and then try to explain why they were unfounded. Nothing helped. No one could change her thoughts. She developed obsessive-compulsive disorder which exhausted her by trying to keep up with all the rituals this behavior demanded. Nothing could be touched without using a tissue. This went on for years.

Over time the house became delapitated because she wouldn't allow anyone in to repair or fix anything. The pool cracked and filled with weeds. She and her husband were divorced. The only person she had any contact with was her son, Domenic. She lived alone with her dog, sleeping all day and staying up all night.

She wouldn't leave the house to see a doctor for any medical problem. Consequently, when she had to be rushed to the hospital with chest pain, it was too late. She passed away at the age of sixty-seven from a massive heart attack.

Her days of envy and greed had come to an end years ago along with her debilitating illness. However, her daughter, Jessica, had the same traits. She had good teachers in her mother and grandmother.

These traits would have a big impact on her and the rest of the family in the future.

Thirty-Three

Gloria had a busy life taking care of her family. There were the daily chores of cooking, cleaning, baking, and doing laundry. She did a large food shopping once a week with smaller errands on other days. Driving the children to their after-school activities and religious instruction also took a lot of her time. Antonio's job kept him away from home for long days, so she was mostly responsibile for maintaining the household and caring for the children.

They did well in school. The boys became interested in sports, Boy Scouts, and music. Her daughter, Lisa, enjoyed dancing lessons and the drama club. As soon as they turned sixteen, they found part-time jobs to save for college. They had inherited Gloria's good sense and also her sense of humor.

Her oldest son, Antonio, Jr. became an architect eventually starting his own business. He worked in conjunction with his younger brother, Roberto, who was a contractor building many homes, churches and buildings. Lisa became a school teacher on the high school level. When her youngest went to school, Gloria went back to work to help support the family. Gloria would feel resentment toward Angelina when she would tell everyone Gloria preferred working rather than staying home to take care of her children.

Etta's children, Domenic and Jessica were brought up mostly by their grandmother. The majoity of their lives they had to deal with their mother's phobias. In spite of this, they did well in school and managed to make some friends even though they couldn't bring them home. It also helped being very well-off financially.

Jessica, like her mother and grandmother, never had enough. She felt good knowing she always had more than her cousin, Lisa. She had many boyfriends growing up, to the point of being promiscuous. She would stay with one for a year or two leading them on to the point of getting engaged, then changing her mind and dropping them before marriage. Many were left broken-hearted—one actually had a nervous breakdown. Another ended up in the hospital not knowing who or where he was. She definitely had a power over men. She dropped out of college and held mediocre jobs which she worked for a while but somehow always managed to end up collecting unemployment. Her life was one of working and collecting, working and collecting for years.

Domenic did well in school and became a successful engineer. He was very devoted to his mother and tried to take care of her abnormal needs. He married his high school sweetheart, and they had one son. This relationship gave him some happiness and stability.

For many years Angelina kept pressuring Augustino to build a home on the three acres of land he had purchased so long ago. It was a constant feeling of jealousy to think of her sister Mena's beautiful home. She now had another one in Florida! It was difficult to visit there without envy and wanting one of her own, but newer and better. Her dream mansion with the pillars in front (one worthy of her presence), ended up being a one-room cabin with no facilities or running water. It became a little family retreat on weekends in the summer. This just became another committment for Angelina's children and grandcildren. If they didn't go every Sunday, life wouldn't be worth living with Angelina's guilt trips. After many years of this tradition, her family grew old, her children and especially her grandchildren became bored. There was nothing for them to do there; they wanted to move on. The weekends drifted off until the tradition ended.

Finally, Angelina came to realize she and Augustino, Jr. were too old to build a new home. Her dream mansion with the pillars in front (one worthy of her presence) was not to be. The land lay quiet for a few years.

Gloria's oldest son Antonio, Jr. had married. He approached his grandmother, asking if he could purchase the land to build a home there. With eyes blazing she looked at him as if he had asked for a million dollars. She flatly refused saying that land was to be given to no one but her grandson, Domenic. He was turned away as if he were an unworthy peasant. A few years later, Lisa's husband, Thomas, thought he would take a chance and ask her if he could purchase the land. He was denied for the same reason.

She would never let any of Gloria's children buy that land. Gloria might end up living with one of her children. Then, Gloria would be living where Angelina always wanted to be. What a horrible thought! The only one she would give that land to was her daughter's son, Domenic. In her mind he was the only one worthy of it.

Years later, when she thought it was the right time, she offered the land to Domenic. She couldn't wait for his excited acceptance and profound thanks.

Domenic refused her offer. He didn't want the land. His wife wanted to live where her family and friends were on the other side of the state.

Angelina was dumbfounded. She was deflated. Again her dream for that land had been shattered. She waited a little while hoping Domenic would change his mind. He didn't. She would never offer it to any of Angelina's children. It was eventually sold to a stranger.

Angelina's behavior with her children regarding the land opened old wounds for Gloria. It brought back terrible memories of what Angelina and Augustino, Jr. had done to her and Antonio years ago. It was something she had tried to forget over time to keep peace in the family, but being such a horrific event, it had become impossible.

Thirty-Four

Now Gloria remembered as if it was yesterday what had happened the year Grandpa Pasquale, Sr. died. Since his wife, Carmella had passed on, he had made it known to everyone in the family he wanted to leave the ten stores which housed the tailor shop, to his grandson, Antonio. He wanted to make sure Antonio, because of his handicap, never had to worry about taking care of himself and his family financially. He also had a paid-up insurance policy for him that would pay him so much a month for the rest of his life when he turned twenty-one. Antonio had not taken any payments from it yet, so it was worth ten-thousand dollars. Pasquale, Sr. made out a will stating all these desires. It also stated he had given his son, Augustino and his wife, Angelina, everything he wanted them to have in his lifetime and therefore they were left nothing in the will. So when Pasquale, Sr. passed, he died knowing everything he wanted was taken care of. Or so he thought!

While he was living, he didn't know his son, Augustino, and his daughter, Maria, never made him aware of a loophole in the deed to the property. He was sure when his wife passed on the property was automatically his. He was never told the deed was made out so his wife's half was passed down to her children. This meant Augustino and his sister, Maria, each had a piece of the pie.

Maria and her three children quickly took advntage of this. They swooped down like vultures on Antonio, hired a shark lawyer, and confiscated the ten-thousand dollar insurance plus the rest of their half from the property. They had a ball buying new cars, remodeling their homes and purchasing new clothes.

Augustino and especially Angelina seemed horrified relatives could do this to family. How could they be so vicious not only because their son was handicapped, but his wife was six months pregnant with their third child. They cursed them and hoped they spent all the money on cancer treatments.

Gloria wondered the same thing. How could they? Although wishing someone cancer was too harsh.

Shortly after Antonio had lost most of his assets to these greedy relatives, Gloria received a phone call from Angelina asking her and Antonio to come to their home the following evening for coffee. In all her innocence with her swollen belly preceding her, Gloria went with Antonio the following evening to his parents' home. During the toxic coffee hour, Augustino, prompted by Angelina, choked out words saying they would also like their share of the property. Antonio showed no emotion as if he knew what was coming, but Gloria was shocked and dumbfounded. What kind of parents would ask a handicapped son and his pregnant wife for money when they knew how much he had already lost and how little was left? What kind of merciless people were they?

When the fact was brought up how little was left to share, Augustino suggested they could take out a mortgage on the property. Gloria couldn't believe what was happening. She left that evening and cried for days. She worried about how this trauma would affect her unborn child.

The in-laws had already hired a lawyer. Antonio was asked to sign an agreement for payment to them. Gloria wanted to know what the agreement was, but every time she went with Antonio to the meeting, it would be cancelled.

Gloria took it upon herself to try and plead their case. She approached Angelina on one of the cancelled meeting nights. She told Angelina she had a copy of Pasquale, Sr.'s will. He stated he had given them everything he had wanted them to have in his lifetime. He didn't want them to have anything else.

Angelina whirled around, looked at Gloria with fire in her eyes and spit out the words, "I want something for my other two children." There was no reasoning with a greedy, wild woman.

Eventually Gloria found out Antonio had signed some agreement with his parents stating he had to pay them so much a month for as long as they both lived. Everything was done secretly. Gloria was told nothing. She resented this, was terribly hurt her husband had such little regard for her and wouldn't defend her to his parents.

When Augustino passed a few years later, the payments continued to Angelina for many more years until her death. Even when times were hard and the property was going to be auctioned off because of unpaid taxes, she didn't care. She still wanted her monthy payment. Either it was Angelina's dying wish or it was in the original agreement, but Antonio would never put Gloria's name on the property. If she ever mentioned it, he would go into a rage.

This had been the hardest, most heart-wrenching experience from which Gloria had to recuperate. She couldn't conceive of parents taking from one of their children especially under such circumstances. All the parents she knew in her family were loving, caring people who couldn't do enough for their children. From then on she held a deep resentment for her in-laws and her husband. She was brought up to always "keep the peace." With difficulty she tried. She also couldn't deny her children from knowing their grandparents.

That is why this latest incident with Angelina denying Gloria's children from buying the land to build a home brought back the painful thoughts of what had happened years ago. Angelina's greed and jealousy were still very much alive.

Would the day ever come when Angelina would be brought to justice for all her deeds? Would it ever happen? Gloria might be disappointed. Or would she?

Thirty-Five

Angelina was never happy with the settlement. She wanted more for her son, Cosimo and her daughter's children. It made her ill to think Gloria's children would inherit the entire property. If Gloria ever needed financial help, she was sure her children would come to her rescue with money from there. She would get to share in the profits. Unbearable thought! There was nothing she could do to prevent it. It gnawed at her like a dog with a bone.

Augustino continued to work in the tailor shop until he became ill with lung cancer. The business was sold, but as was written in the contract with Antonio years ago, the money from whoever rented that shop would be given to the Rossis for the rest of their lives. Gloria, just becoming aware of this, thought they had made a better deal than the other vultures in the family.

After Augustino's passing, Angelina now depended on Cosimo to take care of her. She made a will leaving the house to him. She knew he would leave it to her daughter's children, Domenic, and, Jessica, because they were almost like his own.

Even though Cosimo was very attentive to her every need, Angelina still wanted her oldest son, Antonio, to also do his duty toward her. He would stop by her house on the way home from work almost every night. Sometimes she would have prepared what she called a "nourishing meal" waiting for him. He felt obligated to eat it even though he knew Gloria had dinner waiting for him. He couldn't disappoint his mother because he knew she wanted to feel he was "well nourished." Gloria's meals just couldn't add up. When he finally sat at the dinner table at home, he would force himself to eat a little, and then say for some reason he wasn't very hungry. Gloria knew too well what had transpired.

Gloria worked all week and Saturday was her busy day to catch up on household chores. She could have used some help. Since her children had weekend jobs, she would have liked to rely on Antonio. It wasn't to be.

With the excuse of having an early doctor's appointment every Saturday morning, Angelina would confiscate Antonio for the whole day. The doctor would be followed by shopping, errands, having lunch and anything else she could think of. Gloria inquired if Angelina could get a later doctor's appointment so Antonio could help her with some of the morning chores. She was informed by Antonio this was the only appointment available for her. Gloria found out this wasn't true. Just another one of Angelina's games.

Gloria's birthday was coming soon. The one bright spot in her life was her daughter, Lisa, who was expecting her first child. Gloria was ready to become a grandmother and hoped the baby would be born on her birthday.

She would celebrate her birthday with not only joy but tragedy.

Thirty-Six

Gloria's daughter, Lisa, had started her labor pains early in the morning. She finally decided to go into the hospital around eleven o'clock. Now it was nearing four in the afternoon and Gloria hadn't heard any news. She was getting anxious. Her husband was at work and should be home by six and they would be able to visit Lisa at the hospital. By five o'clock Gloria couldn't wait any longer. She called the hospital to inquire about her daughter. The woman who answered informed her Lisa had given birth to a boy about three hours ago and questioned why she she hadn't been called. Gloria was relieved and happy but did wonder why her son-in-law never let them know. She had worried so long needlessly. She found out later he was so engrossed in the baby he forgot to call.

Now Gloria anxiously waited for her husband to come home so she could tell him the wonderful news. They could go to the hospital and see their new grandson and daughter.

Two hours went by. Antonio was still not home. She was worried. Where was Antonio? This was not like him to be so late!

The phone rang, shaking Gloria out of her worrisome thoughts. She answered. A woman was calling from Memorial Hospital. Her daughter was in General Hospital, so why this call? The woman went on to say her husband had been in an automobile accident and she should come immediately. Gloria's brain couldn't process this news. She had been focused on being happy about her grandson. She started to shake. She drove to the hospital never remembering how she got there. Hopefully Antonio would be all right.

The doctor was waiting for her. When she saw the look on his face she knew something was terribly wrong. How badly had Antonio been hurt? She could see the doctor talking but her body had gone numb. Her ears had shut down. She saw the doctor's lips say "I'm sorry." She didn't want to hear the rest. She felt faint. A nurse came and put her arm around Gloria. As if from far away in a tunnel Gloria heard the doctor's voice say, "He didn't make it."

Gloria was sure this was a bad dream. It wasn't happening. This couldn't be happening. She would go home now. Antonio would be there. They would go see their daughter and new grandson at the hospital. She was helped to a chair. She sat in a coma-like state, not seeing, not hearing.

Someone came to her and asked if there was anyone she would like to call. Somehow she came to her senses long enough to give her two sons' names and phone numbers.

When they arrived the three clung to each other not saying a word. Then the time came when they had to see Antonio. They were brought to the morgue in the basement of the hospital. Antonio's body lay on a slab covered with a sheet. When uncovered it was very evident how badly he had been injured. They wept uncontrollably.

After leaving Antonio, they spoke with a police officer who had been called to the scene of the accident. He told them Antonio had been hit crossing an intersection. According to witnesses, a car with four teenagers came barreling down the cross street so fast he never made it to the other side. They hit him broadside. The car spun around and toppled into a ditch. He must have been killed instantly.

Gloria's sons offered to stay the night with her but she wanted to be alone. She had to clear her head and gather strength for the family.

Tomorrow she would visit her daughter, gently break the news about her father, and take some joy in her new grandson.

What was going to happen next? How could she ever be prepared for the days ahead? Who would be the one to tell Angelina?

Thirty-Seven

After saying goodnight to Gloria, Antonio Jr. and Roberto went to the Rossi's home to deliver the sad news. They told Cosimo first and left him with the burden of telling Angelina.

On being told Angelina was devastated. She walked around the house sobbing and moaning uncontrollably. It was a nightmare. It couldn't be true. How could she go on without her Antonio? Cosimo was a good son, but he didn't have the strength of character like Antonio. She would be lost without him. She tried to find some way to blame Gloria for his death but had to admit she was not responsible. Now Gloria's children would own all that property. Gloria would be the sole owner of her home. Being upset about that almost overcame the sadness of losing Antonio.

The funeral was planned with only three calling hours. The burial was private for family only. It was especially sad for Lisa. Her father's death overshadowed her happiness for her newborn son. He would never know his grandfather.

As usual, when someone passes away, family and friends are very solicitous of the bereaved and offer their condolences and help. This was true with Gloria. Food and flowers were delivered to her home. Friends called wanting to help in any way. Family came to visit offering to stay if she wanted company. The concern was overwhelming for about two weeks. Then, as usual, everything quieted down. Everyone went back to their lives. Gloria was now alone.

She continued to work at the publishing company. Weekends she went to Lisa's to help with the baby. Her grandson, Daniel, brought so much joy into her life. He was a happy, healthy baby. Now she could also distance herself somewhat from Angelina which was a relief. A short time after Daniel was born, her sons and their wives brought more grandchildren into the family. It seemed as though babies were being born every year. This was a wonderful gift for Gloria. She found happiness and fulfillment in helping with her four grandsons and two granddaughters. Life was good.

Cosimo, now being the only son, was completely bound to taking care of his mother. There was absolutely no way out for him. Angelina felt secure knowing Cosimo would take care of her until her dying day.

Cosimo knew what his mother expected of him, but he had plans of his own.

Thirty-Eight

Cosimo was now responsible for taking care of Angelina and maintaining the houseold. He lived a boring existence going to work every day and coming home to the constant whining complaints from his mother. She was never satisfied. It was never enough. She couldn't be pleased. He never was a big eater, but she continued making what she called "nourishing meals" and getting annnoyed when he didn't eat enough. It gave him an upset stomach. He would develop one of his painful headaches. He just wanted to be left alone to live an independent life. It was impossible under these circumstances.

His sister Etta's daughter, Jessica, visited often to see how her grandmother was being cared for. She became another problem for him to deal with. He found her to be a replica of his sister and his mother. Figuring she and her brother were going to inherit the house from him, she was already evaluating the worth of its contents. She would ask Cosimo if she could have some of the valuable figurines, vases and accessories since Angelina wasn't using them anymore. She would ask in the same whiny tone as his mother to make him feel guilty if he refused. He resented these requests and hated himself for not being able to say no. He felt trapped between these two greedy, selfish women.

Angelina had started to lose her mental faculties, became weak, and lost much of her eyesight causing her to fall frequently. She couldn't be left alone. When the doctor advised Cosimo his mother should be placed in a nursing home, he didn't hesitate for a minute. He was relieved.

Cosimo went to visit his mother every day for the first year she was in the nursing home. She was failing, but slowly. He couldn't keep up the pace, so his visits became less frequent. For him the visits had become dreaded sessions of whines, complaints and demands always leaving him with those deep feelings of guilt. It was almost three years before Angelina took her last breath.

Cosimo now really felt a great sense of relief. Almost seventy years old he could finally be his own person. He enjoyed the freedom to make his own decisions and live his life with no committments. His headaches disappeared.

After a few short years of freedom, he started to get dizzy spells and had trouble walking. He went to several doctors, but none could come up with a definite diagnosis.

Jessica, knowing of his problem, started coming by almost every day. With the excuse of helping, she became very aggressive. She was completely involved with his illness keeping track of his doctor's appointments and insisting he take medications even when they didn't agree with him. She became a watchdog over his entire life to the point of being obnoxious. Every time she would do an errand or drive him to a doctor's appointment, she would look for a handout. The greedy gene had definitely been passed down from mother to daughter. At this point he just wanted her to go away and leave him alone. It wasn't to be.

Her grandmother had assured Jessica Cosimo was leaving the house to her and her brother, Domenic when he passed on. Therefore, she felt she had the right to come there as often as she liked. Her brother didn't need or want the house, so she was sure he would deed his half to her. It would be hers alone!

Cosimo had become very resentful of Jessica. Besides always expecting to be paid for whatever she did, she had gone through the house on her many visits and helped herself to most of her grandmother's fine jewelry. Lisa could get the cheap leftovers. Something of value always disappeared after one of her visits.

Cosimo was aware of what was going on. He didn't say anything to Jessica about the situation, but he was thinking seriously about a decision he had to make. Jessica's aggressive and contolling behavior made him very stressed causing his condition to become worse. His headaches had started to return. She had taken the place of his mother.

He knew Angelina had expected him to leave the house to Jessica and Domenic upon his death. For once in his life he was going to go against what his mother expected of him. It would give him a great sense of liberation. Jessica would get the shock of her life. The only drawback would be he wouldn't have the satisfaction of seeing it.

Thirty-Nine

While Cosimo was still able to drive, he had to make an important trip without Jessica's knowledge. She already knew too
much of his business. He didn't want her to know where he was going
today. Jessica was expecting she and her brother were going to inherit
his house. Cosimo had other ideas. He didn't like her greedy, aggressive attitude. She had always gotten everything she ever wanted. He
didn't want her to have his house. Her brother, Domenic had been a
hard worker all his life. He was well off and it wouldn't bother him
if he didn't inherit the house. Jessica had never worked steadily. She
was always turning to others in the family for handouts.

Gloria's children had always been the underdogs. He knew how
his mother favored his sister's children. How she hated to see Gloria
get anything of value. It was so unfair, and yet Gloria and her children
had never caused any problems and had remained respectful toward
them. Also, Gloria was the only one in the family who had been kind
to his ex-wife, Sylvia. They had become friends among all the ene-
mies. Now it was time for the tables to be turned.

He drove to his lawyer's office and drew up a new will. He wanted
to leave his home to Gloria's children. For the first time in his life
he did something he wanted to do. Angelina and Augustino would

never have forgiven him. He didn't give a damn. He drove home with a smile on his face and deep satisfaction in his soul. He didn't even have a headache. When he went to bed that night he felt at peace with his decision. He could just imagine how Jessica would react when she found out what he had done. Thankfully he wouldn't be around to face her anger and scorn.

That night he was awakened by a loud thumping noise. Could it be Angelina turning over in her grave? He smiled, rolled over, and fell back to sleep.

In spite of all Angelina's and Augustino's plotting and scheming over the years to prevent Gloria and her children from owning any of "their" property, the plans had backfired. With Cosimo's latest decision, Gloria and her children would now become owners of all the Rossi's property. It was a true redemption. An innocent redemption!

The best redemption of all was still to come!

Forty

One year after Cosimo's passing, Jessica had not yet recovered from the shock and emotional upheaval of finding out she and her brother had not inherited his home. She couldn't conceive of what had gone wrong. Why would he leave the house to Gloria's children? Something crooked must have taken place. It would take her a long time to get over this. However, she was in for an even bigger shock that would send her reeling.

About two years after Antonio's death, Gloria attended her fiftieth high school reunion. It was fun to get reacquainted with whoever was left in her graduating class. A most pleasant surprise was seeing Edmond Conti again. There had always been a close connection between them. They had a lot in common, took the same classes, had the same interests, often ate lunch together, and had interesting conversations. After graduating they had each gone their separate ways. Now he seemed equally pleased to see her.

They picked up their conversation where they had left off years ago as if it were only the other day. After spending almost the whole evening catching up, when it was time to leave they agreed to keep in touch. From that evening a strong relationship developed. They found themselves falling deeply in love. Since they both had lost their mates, and were not so young anymore, they didn't want to waste time. They wanted to be together permanently. Eight months into their relationship they were married in a small, quiet ceremony with only their immediate families present.

They both owned a home and lived alone. They had a plan. They would sell their homes and build a new one for themselves to enjoy. Edmond had bought three acres of land in the country years ago from a woman named Angelina Rossi. He had wanted to build a home for his wife, but she passed away before it could be done. Now he wanted to build a home there for Gloria. He wanted Gloria to design whatever style home she desired. Talk about redemption!

When Jessica heard about their plans, she went completely spastic. She never fully recovered.

It took one year for the house Gloria designed to be completed. She and Edmond now lived in an elegant home with pillars in front (worthy of her presence).

The first night they slept there, they were awakened by a loud thumping sound—probably the house settling. They kissed, turned over, and went back to sleep.

The End

Made in the USA
Middletown, DE
14 October 2021